STEEPLE HILL BOOKS

Steeple
Hill®

D1057442

ISBN 0-373-78511-9

SWEET DEVOTION

Copyright © 2004 by Felicia L. Mason

This edition published by arrangement with Steeple Hill Books.

® and TM are trademarks of Steeple Hill Books, used under license. Trademarks indicated with ® are registered in the United States Patent and Trademark Office, the Canadian Trade Marks Office and in other countries.

Visit us at www.steeplehill.com

Printed in U.S.A.

Praise for
#1 Blackboard Bestselling Author

FELICIA
MASON

"Mason is a superb storyteller...she creates magic."
—*Publishers Weekly*

"[Mason] places the Christian theme front and center
while also making room for a touching portrait
of human desires and frailties."
—*Booklist*

"Felicia Mason...will make the reader sigh,
cry, then shout for joy at the triumphant,
healing power of true love."
—*Romantic Times*

This book is for all of the Ambers
who seek shelter, peace and hope.

A portion of the proceeds of this book
is being donated to Transitions Family
Violence Services, an organization
that supports women and children in crisis.

✑ Chapter One ✑

Armed with a carving knife, Amber Montgomery took cover as a metal folding chair hurtled her way. The chair crashed against the edge of a white-draped carving table, taking out the end of the serving station where she'd been carving beef at the Wayside Revelers' Annual Dinner Dance.

She watched in horror as eight pounds of beets splattered to the floor sending deep red beet juice splashing up and out like a demented geyser.

She'd known, of course, that taking this catering job carried a certain amount of risk. The Wayside Revelers tended to revel a bit too much at their functions. But after their last fiasco at the VFW hall, Amber thought they'd mellowed and would be on their best behavior tonight.

That, obviously, wasn't the case.

She didn't know how this melée started, but she needed to—

"Watch out!" someone yelled.

Amber ducked just a moment before another chair came within inches of taking *her* out.

This was getting personal!

She jumped up. "Hey, I'm the caterer. Why are you attacking me?"

But no one heard her or paid any attention. They were too busy destroying the hall and themselves—and having a great time doing so. The scene in front of her looked like a barroom brawl in the wild wild West. Except, this wasn't the eighteen-hundreds frontier. It was peaceful little Wayside, Oregon, population 17,800, in the twenty-first century.

Over the commotion, Amber heard what sounded like police sirens. Help was on the way!

Maybe she could salvage the trays of lemon meringue tarts—six hours of work. Amber inched toward the desserts, but someone else spied them at the same time. An elderly man grabbed one in each hand and smiled.

"Don't you have any respect for food?" she demanded.

Unmindful of the scene playing out behind him, the man shook his head, grinned a toothless smile and aimed.

"Don't you dare!" Amber said, holding a hand up in front of her face.

"Lighten up, honey," he said. "It's just a pastry."

And then her own lemon meringue hit her in the face. Amber shrieked and whirled around—

"Hold it right there."

With one hand Amber wiped pie from her face. She cleared her vision enough to see the pie thrower scuttle off to the side and disappear into the crowd. She wiped away more meringue and the shadow in front of her came into focus, the details registering. Tall, with broad shoulders, a slim waist and feet planted apart, he scowled at her. A very big, very threatening cop stood not three feet away.

"You're under arrest, lady."

"Me? What did I do? I'm the one being attacked. Arrest one of them," she demanded, waving the carving knife toward the Revelers now merrily flinging the rest of her lemon tarts at each other.

The cop didn't spare a glance at the havoc being wrought behind him. "Drop the knife now."

Amber tensed at the tone. Then she looked up at the cop. His eyes glinted and she realized that his hand hovered near his revolver.

"What knife?"

He took a menacing step forward, and Amber whimpered. The carving knife she'd forgotten she clutched in her hand clattered to the floor. In the next moment, the cop was all over her. He grabbed her arm, yanking it around her back.

"You're hurting me."

He didn't answer. Instead, she felt the cold steel of handcuffs clamp on her wrist.

Something snapped in her then, and Amber fought. A

fragment of the self-defense she'd been taught flickered through her. She kicked out at him. "No! You can't do this. I won't let you do this…"

One of her kicks connected and she heard his intake of breath. Her small victory, however, was short-lived. He held her tightly and secured the other wrist.

"Lady, if you don't settle down," he said, his voice a deceptively calm growl, "I'm going to add resisting arrest to your charges."

It wasn't so much what he said as the way the words sounded that got to her. They held a rumbled warning of coming pain. She knew that tone, knew what would happen to her if she defied him again. She'd tried to fight. She'd tried to remember she didn't have to be a victim. She'd also tried to remember how to defend herself.

But he had the physical advantage of height and weight and strength. Resistance *was* futile, she realized. Why did it always have to be this way?

Amber closed her eyes and surrendered to the inevitable.

The handcuffed woman went limp, and Paul had to move fast to catch her before she hit the floor.

Police Chief Paul Evans commanded a force of forty sworn officers and a full complement of dispatchers, secretaries and other civilians whose job it was to maintain the peace in Wayside. He'd been warned that the Wayside Revelers had a tendency to get out of hand at their events. So he'd been on patrol in the vicinity of the community center.

When he heard first a shout and then breaking glass, he'd called for backup and rushed in, just in time to have a small, blond beauty threaten him with a wicked-looking blade.

Even now, with the hellion subdued at his side, his officers swarmed the building rounding up rabble-rousers.

He turned to call one of the officers—

Thwack!

A mound of potatoes au gratin hit his forehead. Paul spotted the culprit, a little old man who quickly ditched the serving spoon he'd used as a missile launcher. The man then snatched up a serving tray lid and used it as a shield against the lemon tarts hurled his way.

"Jones!" Paul bellowed.

The cop sprinted forward.

"You there," Paul ordered the old man. "Stop it."

The devilish gleam in the elderly man's eyes was replaced by an expression of innocence and fake senility. "Me?"

"Yeah, you."

Dragging along a remarkably subdued knife wielder, Paul unlocked a second pair of cuffs.

"You're arresting me?"

"That's right, sir."

"Hot diggity!" The little man stepped quickly to don the cuffs, showing pretty amazing dexterity for someone his age. Paul put him at close to eighty.

"Take these two out to my squad car," he said to the young officer. "I'll go round up some more of them." He wiped his brow, shook potato goo from his hand and glared at the old man who was still grinning at him.

"Assaulting an officer could earn you some jail time, sir."

"As long as you have cable, that's fine by me. I like to watch wrestling."

"I'll just bet you do," Paul muttered, walking away and stepping around a huge puddle of beets. The whole place was a wreck.

In the police car, Amber stared out the window, her face an expressionless mask.

"Isn't this fun?" the little man asked.

It took a moment for the question to sink in and for Amber to comprehend that the pain hadn't kicked in yet. She turned toward the voice, expecting to see her tormentor. Instead, she came eye-to-eye with an elf. Her eyes widened and her mouth, a thin line, began to tremble.

The man looked alarmed. "Aw, please don't be mad. It was just a little pastry. It didn't hurt, did it?"

Amber opened her mouth but no words came forth. Her tongue felt like sandpaper. She blinked once. Then again. And then the tears she'd hoped to hold back started to fall.

The man moved as if to comfort her, then, too late, remembered his hands were cuffed. He almost toppled into her lap. Amber squealed and pressed her back to the door. The little man righted himself.

"Oh, honey. It's not that bad. Really. They'll just take us down, do some fingerprints and then give us a good lecture. I missed last year's dinner-dance, but that's what I'm told happened."

Amber just moaned.

To the casual observer, the Main Street district of Wayside, Oregon, might look a whole lot like Mayberry, R.F.D., but the police bureau was a reminder that crime happened in the town just like it did in every other American locality.

Once inside the large oak and cherry doors of the police bureau, it was apparent to any visitor that despite Wayside's size, it had a state-of-the-art police department, fully equipped to handle any twenty-first century criminal activity and to protect the town's citizens from such.

A long line of Revelers was herded past the intake desk and into lockup.

Amber stood in the midst of about thirty-five food-stained wretches, most of them incredibly self-satisfied over this bonus extension of their night's festivities.

"My name's Silas," someone said.

Amber looked beside her. There stood her pie thrower, the little man from the police car. Having recovered enough to speak, Amber opened her mouth to give him what-for. But a voice boomed out over the general hubbub, drowning out her first words.

"Listen up, people."

Amber's skin prickled at the voice. She turned toward

the voice and got another jolt when she looked at the man who'd cuffed and arrested her.

"My name's Paul Evans and I'm the police chief here,"

"Hi, Chief Evans." A couple of the Revelers called out the cheery greeting.

"Welcome to Wayside," the little man at Amber's side hollered.

Amber watched the big cop shake his head in bemusement. She rubbed her wrists. Though the handcuffs had been removed she still felt the weight of the shackles on her spirit. Taking a much-needed deep breath, Amber fought for the calm she knew she could find if she just took it slow. *Keep it light,* she coached herself. One breath at a time.

"We'll be processing each one of you. After that, you're free to go until your court date."

"What about the lecture about being responsible citizens?" one of the Revelers asked.

The cop folded his arms across his chest. Amber watched muscles bunch and constrict, the blue fabric of his uniform pulled taut. Her study of the man missed no detail. From the black hiking boots at his feet, to the gleaming hardware on his gun belt.

His face matched the rest of him. Clean-shaven, angular. She paused at his eyes. Something wasn't right about his eyes. A deep, almost piercing blue, they fit his face, but... Amber tilted her head a fraction, getting another view. At just that second, his gaze connected with hers.

She caught her breath.

He watched her for a moment, then turned his attention back to the group. "You want a lecture about acting like six-year-olds? The community center is completely trashed thanks to your food fight. Who's in charge of you people?"

The crowd in lockup parted. Amber edged forward so she was near the front.

"I don't belong in here," she said. "You've made a mistake."

Paul's eyes narrowed in on her.

"About you, lady, there was no mistake."

"I'm the grand marshal," a man said, stepping forward and poking his chest out.

If it hadn't been for the meringue in his hair, the potatoes on his tie and a missing shoe, he might have passed for "grand."

Chuckling at the assembly, a couple of cops walked up behind the police chief, surveying the mass in lockup.

"What are you doing here, Amber?" Sergeant Caleb Jenkins asked.

"Caleb. Thank God." Relief poured through Amber. "That's the same thing I've been trying to find out. That lug head you call a police chief hauled me in here."

People behind her snickered.

A muscle flickered angrily in Paul's jaw. Though locked bars separated them, Amber stepped back.

"Lug head?"

"Uh," Caleb started. "I, uh... He's not a..." The sergeant didn't meet her gaze, focusing instead on something on his boots.

"There's been some kind of mix-up, Chief," the sergeant said, marshaling his vocabulary and coming to her defense. "This is Amber Montgomery. She's not a Reveler. She's a caterer."

Paul didn't look convinced of her innocence. "You threatened me with a knife."

Amber glared up at him, not letting the physical disparity of their heights dissuade her. "I am a *caterer.* If you'd done any kind of police work, you'd know that that was a carving knife. But how could you do any real police work—you were too busy shoving me around."

Amber thrust her wrists in front of him. "Look." Two bruises marred her pale skin.

Paul looked horrified. "What happened to you? Did somebody in the cage do that to you?"

"No, *Chief* Evans. You did. And you better believe that I'm filing a formal complaint."

She whirled back toward Caleb. "Who hires the police chief?"

"Uh." He looked from Amber to Paul. "Uh…"

"The mayor," Paul supplied.

Just then a commotion in the hallway interrupted them. The main doors burst open. Wayside's mayor strode in, followed by a reporter and a photographer from the *Wayside Gazette* and a frantic-looking Haley Brandon-Dumaine.

"Amber!"

"Paul," the mayor bellowed. "What is going on in here?"

It took a good ten minutes to sort through what had happened.

"I'm pretty disappointed with you, Randall," the mayor told the Revelers' grand marshal. "I thought you all learned your lesson the last time."

The Revelers' last dinner-dance had resulted in a lifetime ban from the VFW hall.

"Some of us weren't there then," Silas called out.

It took a while, but on the mayor's word and that of several longtime police officers, Amber was released from lockup. Haley stood with Amber as she signed the requisite forms.

"Ms. Montgomery, I'm truly sorry. It was an honest mistake," Paul said, approaching them.

Amber's derisive snort clearly said she wasn't buying it.

"Will you let me formally apologize?"

Amber spun around. "You've got a lot of nerve, mister. First you yank me around like I'm some kind of rag doll. Now you think you can just make nice and I'll forget about the way you treated me. Never again," she said. "You'll be hearing from my lawyer."

Those were fine words coming from someone who didn't even know a lawyer, let alone have one.

Amber's dramatic exit from the police station sapped the rest of her energy. By the time they got to Haley's car, Amber felt like a rag doll that had not only been yanked around and dragged across the ground but also run through a washing machine.

"Are you all right?" Haley asked.

Amber nodded, but she stared out the passenger-side window of Haley's car. "I need to get my stuff. My van is still at the community center."

Haley winced. "I don't think you'll be able to get it. At least not tonight. Chief Evans isn't letting anyone near there until they get photos of all the damage. When I drove by, your van was inside the crime scene tape."

"Great, just great. How am I supposed to make my deliveries tomorrow?"

"You can take my car if you need it. I'll have Matt drop me off at school." Haley stopped at a red light and reached a hand out to her cousin. "Amber, I'm worried about you."

Amber didn't meet her concerned gaze. "I'm fine," she said, trying to convince herself. "And I'm not going to have a breakdown, if that's what you're worried about."

The two women rode in silence for a moment. Then Amber, in a voice that was steady and strong, said, "The only thing on my mind is making that cop pay for what he did to me."

Haley glanced at her. "Which cop, Amber? The one here, or the one who hurt you in L.A.?"

ᴁ Chapter Two ᴁ

Paul Evans pulled into his driveway after a long shift. In his three months in Wayside, this had been the first time he'd experienced any rowdiness in the small town.

And he'd take what amounted to a massive food fight over the rough and tumble of the place he'd come from. Wayside, Oregon, was a world and a culture away from Los Angeles.

He'd been given a heads-up about the Wayside Revelers, so he'd been expecting a need to cruise by their dinner-dance during his patrol shift.

The Revelers were all supposed to be retirees, or at least card-carrying members of the AARP. One in particular, however, didn't fit that profile. Paul hadn't been prepared for the fiery beauty who stood up to him brandishing a knife.

How was he supposed to have known she was the

caterer? Her eyes flashed and she looked as if she were out for blood—his in particular. In the evidence room, he'd taken a look at that knife again. Carving knife or not, it could have done some damage had it truly been used as a weapon.

On the drive home, just one thing stuck with Paul, though, nicking his conscious, pestering his peace of mind, making him doubt what he'd seen with his own two eyes: How could he have grabbed her so hard that he'd left a bruise?

That ate at him like nothing else—even the fact that she kept saying "again." He searched his memory, but couldn't recall arresting her in L.A. Granted, he'd arrested a lot of people in his ten years as a cop on the street there. Maybe she'd been in the number. But surely he'd remember someone who looked like Amber Montgomery—like summer and cornfields and blue skies.

She'd caught his eye, all right.

Not remembering her as a suspect in L.A., however, didn't bother him as much as that bruise on her arm.

The other Revelers tossed food around. Messy, yes. But not necessarily deadly. The knife wielded by Amber Montgomery, well, that piece of business was another story altogether. Despite her objection, the weapon had been bagged, tagged and put into an evidence locker at the police station.

He thought he'd let go of at least some of the wariness and care that had served him well on the LAPD. But apparently, he'd not yet gotten acclimated to Wayside and its considerably lower crime rate.

If a geriatric food fight ranked as serious crime here—serious enough to roust the mayor and get him to police headquarters—Paul had definitely settled in the right place. In a city the size of Los Angeles, only crimes like mass rioting, terrorism or a high-profile celebrity slaying ranked severe enough for top public officials to make an unscheduled appearance at police headquarters.

Yeah, he'd take a food fight any day over what he'd left behind.

Drawing a deep breath, Paul shed the cares of the job in exchange for the role that brought him the greatest sense of satisfaction.

"Hi, Eunice," he said, walking in his front door. He unbuckled his gun belt, locked both the revolver and the belt in a closet, then tucked the key away on the chain he always wore around his neck.

"Well, howdy, Chief. Busy night, huh? I heard the Revelers got out of control again."

He nodded. "You could say that. Thanks for staying with the kids."

She wrapped up the knitting she'd been doing, placed yarn and needles in a large quilted bag at her side. "Not a problem. Sutton and Jonathan are fast asleep, bless their little hearts. You have two fine children there, Chief."

Paul thought so, too. "I hope they didn't wear you out too much."

Eunice pooh-poohed that. "If anything, it's the other way around," she said on a chuckle. "We had fun."

He pulled out his wallet.

"If you hand me any money, Paul Evans, I'm going to be mighty insulted."

"Eunice, I can't let you do this and not pay you."

"You're new to Wayside," she said, patting his hand. "You'll get the hang of the place soon. I left a plate of cookies for you. We made gingerbread men."

Paul smiled. Having Eunice Gallagher living right across the street was a godsend, one of many he'd encountered in Wayside. She was the secretary at Community Christian Church, where he'd transferred his membership shortly after arriving in Wayside. A native of Wayside, she'd all but adopted him and his kids.

He helped her with her coat.

"Eunice, do you know a woman by the name of Amber Montgomery?"

The older lady beamed. "Of course! Everybody knows Amber. Don't tell me you haven't had one of her honey pecan rolls yet."

"Honey pecan rolls?"

Eunice laughed. "Goodness, how in the world have you lived here for three months and not had one of those yet? Tell you what, I'll swing by the inn tomorrow and get you some if they're not sold out by the time I get there. You're in for a treat."

He was still trying to understand. "Wait, so she's the town baker?"

Eunice picked up her knitting bag. "No. She's a gourmet chef. She runs a catering business called Appetizers & More, but most people know her for the honey pecan rolls and her lemon meringue tarts." Eunice smacked her lips. "Talk about delicious."

Since he'd been hit with potatoes and not tarts, Paul couldn't agree or disagree. He thought back to Amber's earlier behavior, though, if she hadn't looked so dazed, he'd have sworn she'd played a tactic used by nonviolent protesters. That going limp bit had been used for decades.

"Shock," he surmised. She had to have been in shock. Law-abiding citizens could be counted on to react in one of two ways—outrage or polite pacifism—while they waited patiently or impatiently—for things to get sorted out.

He'd spent so many years working the violent streets of South-Central L.A. that he'd forgotten about law-abiding citizens. Tonight wasn't the first time he'd had a knife in his face. But it probably was the first time in his law enforcement career that the brandisher hadn't tried to slice him with it.

Paul felt bad—really, really bad—about the bruise he'd put on her arm.

After he watched Eunice cross the street, open her door then flick her front porch light, Paul looked in on his sleeping children. Sutton, whose teddy bear Bentley and rag doll Angel cuddled close to her, looked like an angel herself. Her blond curls spread out over the pillow.

She looked a lot like her mom. Paul's heart constricted at the thought.

He stood watching her for a while. Then he placed a kiss on her head and whispered "I love you" to the sleeping child.

A bathroom connected the two bedrooms, and the doors always remained open. On the countertop sat Wally, another of Sutton's stuffed toys—this one a rainbow fish.

With a small chuckle, Paul greeted Wally. "So you're on the night watch this evening."

Paul walked through to Jonathan's room where lights blazed overhead and at the boy's desk. Sprawled on his twin bed with its cartoon-character sheets, Jonathan had, as usual, kicked all the covers off. Paul tugged the sheet and light blanket up.

The boy stirred. "Izzat you, Unca Pa?"

Paul smiled, easily translating the sleep talk. "Yeah, sport. It's me. I'm home. Go back to sleep."

Jonathan sat up, bleary eyed. "Tried to stay awake. Protect the women."

"I know, sport."

His heart went out to the child. Paul hugged him close, then settled him down and tucked him in. "I'll take over the watch now. All right?"

Jonathan murmured his assent and closed his eyes. Paul leaned down, pressed a kiss to the boy's head, then turned off the lights in the bedroom.

The bathroom lights stayed on at night. Always. They helped chase the bad guys away.

* * *

Amber didn't have an answer to Haley's question. No doubt about it, she'd flashed to Raymond Alvarez tonight, at some point confusing the two men, the two situations. Miles away from her former terror, she thought she'd put it all behind her. Until tonight.

The height, the uniform, the eyes...

She shook her head, again thinking of Paul Evans's eyes. Were they the same deep Mediterranean blue as Raymond Alvarez's? She couldn't remember, but the police chief's were somehow different. Kinder maybe?

No, not kinder, she decided. Compassionate. Though he wore the uniform and carried the gun, Paul Evans's eyes had regarded her with warmth. Raymond's eyes, like his soul, were hollow, devoid of any human warmth or consideration. He was a heartless snake in the grass, and it had taken a long time for her to realize that. Too long.

"Would you like me to stay with you tonight?" Haley asked.

Amber shook her head. If there were any ghosts that needed exorcising, she'd do it alone. "No."

"How about staying over with me and Matt? The bed in the guest room is mucho comfy."

That got a small smile, but Amber shook her head again. "I'm all right." And she truly believed she was. She rubbed her upper arm where the cop had gripped her.

"Maybe we should swing by the hospital and have that looked at."

"It's just a bruise, Haley," Amber said. "I've survived much worse."

There was nothing Haley could say to that.

After Haley dropped her off, Amber let herself into her apartment.

Once before she'd been a victim. Never, ever again. Anger still propelling her, and before the fear kicked in, she drafted a letter demanding an investigation into the unnecessary force used by the police chief of Wayside, Oregon. It felt good, too, to lambaste him in writing for the way he'd manhandled her.

In the morning, she'd mail copies to the mayor, the town council, the editor of the *Wayside Gazette* and the news department at the radio station she listened to. Amber knew that letting off steam in the letter was healthy—a much better response than when she used to pretend that nothing was wrong, that her feelings or her body hadn't been physically violated.

Surveying her handiwork, she nodded, satisfied, then put the letters in envelopes and stamped them. Then, with every light on in her house, Amber sat in a deep chair, arms curled around her legs.

Eventually she fell into a fitful sleep.

Morning came quickly. She ran five miles to get the kinks out of her body and to chase away the shadows of the previous evening. The fresh air of an early Oregon morning did wonders in restoring her self-confidence.

She'd face down this day and whatever it delivered with a new determination, a new purpose.

The lesson of last night, Amber decided, was a test of her commitment to rebuilding her life post-Raymond. It had taken three years—three long, liberating years—to get where she was today. Amber had no intention of letting one bullying police chief bring her down again.

After returning from her run, she showered and tried to shrug off the vestiges of the previous night's trauma. Next to running, which she did at every opportunity, Amber's all-time favorite stress reliever was working in her kitchen. Today she got to do something fun, something she enjoyed. She mixed up the basic dough for sugar cookies and chocolate chip cookies.

Using a light frosting, she decorated the sugar cookies once they were baked, with whimsical designs. It was time to pack up the cookies that were ready. She lined a large basket with a red-and-white gingham cloth and alternated layers of chocolate chip and sugar cookies.

She pulled a clean apron with the logo of her Appetizers & More company out of a drawer. She added a miniature version of it to the stack of stuff she'd need. Then, with basket in hand, she headed outside. That's when she remembered her van wasn't out back where it was supposed to be, but still at the community center. She couldn't very well make deliveries on her bicycle.

Frustrated, Amber returned to her apartment and called Caleb, told him where the extra key was hidden under the tire carrier, and listened to a lecture about leaving a spare key where any common criminal could get it.

"Like we have common criminals in Wayside," she muttered.

"Amber, there *are* criminals here."

"And one of them wears a badge that says 'Police Chief,'" she retorted. "Are you going to get my van or not?"

"Yeah," he mumbled. "I'll get it."

She wasn't about to tell him that, during the bad time, she'd taken up the practice of keeping a key hidden on her vehicle, never knowing if she might have to escape with just the clothes on her back, that spare key her only route to freedom.

It *had* come to that.

Thanks to Police Chief Paul Evans, those memories, ones she'd managed to suppress in order to make it through each day, now lay right on the surface, taunting her again. Reminding her that a woman was never truly safe.

Fifteen minutes later, Caleb drove up in her van, a Wayside squad car behind him. Amber couldn't see who sat behind the wheel.

"Sorry about the inconvenience, Amber."

He smiled a shy smile and handed her the key. "Where you headed today?"

"Over to Sunshine and Rainbows," she told him. "Hold on a sec, I'll be right back." Amber dashed back to her apartment, tucked a couple of cookies in a small waxed paper sleeve, sealed it with one of her company stickers and picked up her cookie basket.

Back downstairs, she handed Caleb the cookie bag.

A big grin split his face. "Thanks, Amber." He glanced back at the squad car. "Do I have to share?"

"These," she said holding up the basket, "are one way for the kids to learn about sharing. So the answer to you is yes."

The cop groaned and Amber laughed. "Thanks for bringing the van over."

"Not a problem. The chief's really sorry about—"

Amber held up a hand. "Don't even mention him in my presence."

Shaking his head, Caleb glanced back at the squad car. "But, Amber, he's a good guy. Really."

She slid open the side door and tucked the cookie basket inside. "If you really want to show me that *you're* a good guy," she said, "you'll help me load up the rest of the van."

Looking over his shoulder again, Caleb shrugged.

Not waiting for an answer from him, she headed back inside to get the two additional deliveries she had to make: one to the Wayside Inn Bed & Breakfast, and the other, a special order, to the Train Depot.

A few minutes later, Caleb slid the tray for the inn into the specially designed rack in the van. "Amber, I really think you should reconsider about Chief Evans."

She faced him, her expression serious. "Caleb, if you want to remain friends, and I hope you do, you'll not mention the police chief or your unfortunate choice of occupation in my presence. Comprende?"

The cop nodded.

"All right, then. I'll see you around."

She left him standing in front of the house where she rented a second-floor apartment.

Caleb went back to the waiting squad car and got in the passenger seat.

"She's still pretty steamed at you, Chief."

"I gathered as much from your frantic waving. What's she doing?"

"Making deliveries. I can't believe you've been here for three months and you haven't had one of her honey pecan rolls." The cop smacked his lips together. "Delicious."

"So I've heard." Paul pulled onto the street to head back to the station. "She shouldn't leave spare keys on her vehicle. That's just inviting trouble."

Caleb broke the sticker seal on his treat and counted his cookies. Two. He glanced at the chief sitting next to him.

"What?" asked Paul.

"I only got two."

"Two what?"

"Cookies. She said I had to share."

"Cookies?" In a flash, Paul knew just where one of her deliveries would be made. For the last month, Sutton and Jonathan had been raving about the Cookie Lady at their after-school program. She came once a week.

From their description—soft and funny, and "she smells good"—that from Jonathan—he'd come to the conclusion that the Cookie Lady was a sixtyish grandmother who spent her retirement baking cookies for the town's kids.

If, as he suddenly suspected, Amber Montgomery was the Cookie Lady...Jonathan was partly right. Paul could claim firsthand knowledge of the soft part. But the Amber he'd met smelled like beets, beef and lemon meringue. And there'd been nothing funny or entertaining about last night.

Breaking off a teeny, tiny bit of chocolate chip cookie from the large treat, Caleb offered it to Paul.

"What's this?"

"Well, she said I had to share. But if she knew you were the person in this car, I don't think she'd want you to have any."

Paul snorted. "You're probably right." He glanced at the sliver. "This is your idea of sharing?"

Caleb bit a piece of his much larger cookie, closed his eyes and moaned. "I'd marry that woman in a heartbeat if she were interested."

That comment earned him a quizzical look.

"She doesn't date."

Paul grinned. "Maybe you're not her type."

Caleb smiled back. "That may be so." He waved the last bite of the first cookie at Paul, then popped it in his mouth. "But I'm the one with the cookies."

✂ Chapter Three ✂

Amber's trademark honey pecan rolls went to the inn, then she dropped off a baker's box filled with miniature versions of the sweet rolls to the Train Depot, a gallery in town that showcased model trains and railroad memorabilia.

Amber's little business was growing. Soon it would be time to consider expanding, maybe finding a space to rent or building a Web site. But she liked being a small, one-woman operation. That way, she didn't have to depend on anyone else. Self-sufficient. That's how she described herself.

And that fit in more ways than one.

Appetizers & More by Amber didn't have any employees. But Amber did have two faithful college students who, for a flat fee and a meal, helped her out with some of the larger events.

"Oh, no!" She'd forgotten to check on Dana last night. She couldn't recall seeing her at the police station. So maybe she'd gotten away before the police roundup.

If she got caught in the dragnet, Dana probably got as much of a kick out of it as that little man Silas.

Amber didn't like or trust cops. The only reason she tolerated Caleb Jenkins was that she'd gotten to know him first as a fellow runner and then as the instructor in a karate class she'd taken shortly after moving to Wayside. It had been almost six months before she found out what he actually did for a living. By then, she'd learned to trust him. A little.

That thought led her right back to Paul Evans, and her mood soured.

The Cookie Lady couldn't greet the kids at Sunshine and Rainbows looking or acting like Oscar the Grouch. So she deliberately forced out of her head all thoughts of a tall, broad cop with steely blue eyes.

At least, that's what she told herself.

But she did make a quick cell call to check on Dana.

"Wasn't that a riot? Those old folks really tore up the place. Hey, what happened to you?"

Amber quickly explained about getting caught in the roundup.

"Well, I'm glad you're okay. I gathered up all the serving utensils and your knife kit. A knife is missing, though. I looked everywhere."

Amber rolled her eyes. Her best—translation, "most expensive"—carving knife was safe and sound...in police custody. "Don't worry. I know where it is."

"Whew, that's a relief. That's the one thing they teach us to guard like Fort Knox."

Amber made a note to get Dana a good wrap the next time she went to her favorite cook's supply store in Portland. Just like barbers and beauticians, every professional chef traveled with a personal kit that carried the tools of the trade. Amber had seen it all used, from heavy-duty toolboxes purchased at hardware stores to carryall bags that looked like sling packs. She preferred wraps that had slots for every knife and easily rolled up.

Of course, that numbskull police chief wouldn't know anything about what a chef needed to do her job. He just made assumptions, and probably would have snatched her kit as evidence if Dana hadn't rescued it. Amber assured Dana she'd swing by the college, pick up her knife kit and give Dana her pay.

"And I'll add a little something extra," she told the young woman. "When I asked you to help, I didn't know I needed to provide combat-duty pay."

Dana laughed. "Hey, I'm not gonna turn it down. I'm a starving college student."

"Starving, eh?"

The plump Dana, who always complained that she gained three pounds every time she worked for Amber, chuckled. "Well, you know. Amber, I can't thank you enough for this opportunity," the college student gushed. "I have a blast when I work for you."

Amber grunted. Seeing her food thrown around like garbage, then being arrested didn't exactly rank in her book of top ten ways to have fun. "Different strokes for different folks, I guess."

On the short drive to Sunshine and Rainbows After-School and After-Care Center, Amber did some deep breathing exercises, trying to center herself again. It didn't work. But when she walked through the doors of the kids' center, her spirit soared.

Delighted squeals and children racing each other to clamp themselves around her legs could do that to a woman.

"Well, hello there! With that kind of welcome maybe I'll have to come here more often."

One child, while clearly excited, hung back from the others. Amber smiled at her. "Hi, Sutton."

The girl beamed, but didn't say anything.

"Come on, you guys, let the Cookie Lady through." Marnie Shepherd shooed kids away. "Why don't you go get your mats and show the Cookie Lady how good little boys and girls greet guests?"

The kids raced off, and Amber laughed. Sutton glanced over her shoulder at Amber. She sent the little girl a three-finger wave.

"You do have a way with them," Amber said to Marnie.

Shaking her head, Marnie smiled. "You'd think they'd never had cookies before. It's good to see you again, Amber."

The two women headed to the area where once a week Amber sat in a rocking chair, read a story to the kids, then passed out cookies from her basket. She took pleasure in the activity and always suspected that she got more out of it than the kids did.

"Hey, I have all but three permission slips back for next week. And," Marnie added, pleased with herself, "there are four parent volunteers to make sure things stay under control."

"I'm impressed," Amber said. "But remember, we're not really baking. The no-bake cookies are pretty easy. It's mostly just mixing ingredients. We won't need that much help."

"Oh, yes, we will."

Amber shrugged. What did she know about kids? "If you say so."

She paused at the aquarium, mesmerized as the fish in the huge tank swam by. Watching tropical fish could be the most calming thing.

A little boy approached. "Come on, Cookie Lady. We're all ready."

"Well then, let's get started."

Amber followed her young escort to the section of the room designated with a colorful banner proclaiming it Story Corner.

Some of the children tried to put their mats in front of others to claim a seat closer to the rocker where she'd sit. Amber smiled as one of the aides got them all settled, assuring everyone that they would be able to both see and hear the story. Looking over them, Amber's gaze fell on Sutton.

She liked Sutton. The quiet little girl with the strawberry-blond curls reminded Amber of herself at that age. All pigtails and wide eyes, Sutton never said a lot, but Amber could tell she was bright; the child's eyes never missed a thing and she'd unselfconsciously laugh at a joke until someone noticed her, then hide her face. The girl's older brother always hovered near, keeping her in sight like a miniature bodyguard.

Amber smiled, wryly this time, for that, too, was a familiar scene. Her own older brother had always assumed the role of champion and protector—whether she had wanted him to or not. When she'd really needed a protector, however, Kyle had been half a world away. She'd neither seen nor heard from him in about five, maybe six years, and since she remained incommunicado with her parents, who probably knew his whereabouts, there existed little chance of finding him.

As she watched the boy—she believed Jonathan was his name—bend over and tie the little girl's shoes, Amber realized just how much she missed Kyle. Moisture filled her eyes and she blinked rapidly to dispel the tears that threatened.

"Amber?"

"Huh?" She wiped at her eyes and glanced over at Marnie.

"Are you all right?"

Amber nodded, then forced a grin. "Fit as a fiddle and feeling fine."

After placing the cookie basket on a low table, Amber took her seat in the rocker and addressed the children. It was an effort to dispel thoughts of Kyle, but she put a real smile on her face and in her voice.

"Today, Miss Shepherd tells me that my helper will be from the five-year-old class. All the five-year-olds, raise your hands."

About eight little arms shot up in the air.

"Oh, my. I'm the lucky one today. So who will it be?"

"Me! Me!"

Marnie stepped up with a paper bag. "Have a seat, Junior. You know the rules."

Each time the Cookie Lady—or any special guest—paid a visit, one child got to be the helper. The special role rotated among the age groups. All the children wanted to be the helper when the Cookie Lady came. Being her assistant meant getting to wear a special apron as well as receiving an extra cookie.

Marnie shook the bag with the five-year-olds' names in it. Then, with her eyes squeezed shut, Amber stuck her hand in the bag and pulled out a slip of paper. She read out the name written in blue crayon: "Sutton."

The little girl's eyes widened. Then, suddenly unsure, she scuttled back. Her brother was right there.

"It's okay, Sutton. You get to be the helper today."

Amber held out a hand. "I have the Cookie Lady apron for you to wear. Would you like that?"

The girl nodded.

Amber held it out. Sutton got up and put her hand in Amber's. The two smiled at each other as they donned their aprons.

Sometimes in addition to passing out cookies, the helper turned pages in the storybook. Amber whispered something to Sutton, who nodded and whispered something back. Then Amber started reading the story.

Today's tale came straight from the barnyard and required a lot of animal sound effects.

Paul dropped Caleb off at the police station, then continued his patrol of the town. Even though he served as chief of police, a job largely administrative in a town the size of Wayside, Paul had put himself in the patrol shift rotation after he got acclimated to the day-to-day job as chief. He wanted to get better acquainted with the Wayside community and its residents, and there was no better way to do that than work patrol. And in East Wayside, a section more prone to crime, he walked a beat, getting to know people.

Today, though, since the center was near his patrol area, he decided to swing by to see if Caleb's cookie lady was indeed the Amber he'd met last night. Sutton and Jonathan raved about the Cookie Lady. Paul wanted to see for himself. Maybe last night had been an aberration.

Where his kids were concerned, Paul had to admit to being an overly protective and cautious parent. He'd checked out several programs before choosing Sunshine and Rainbows. Three different people, including Eunice, had recommended it. It was going well, so far. He'd even signed up to be a parent volunteer when they had a cooking lesson next week.

Paul strode into Sunshine and Rainbows and greeted the aide who manned the front desk.

"Hi, Chief Evans. Did you come to check on the kids?"

Paul took off the Wayside Police Bureau cap he wore and tucked it in a pocket. "I was just in the area," he said, feeling a little guilty since he'd deliberately put himself in the area. "Thought I'd stop by. How's everything going?"

"Just fine," she said with a grin. "The Cookie Lady is here."

Paul bit back a smile. This grown woman sounded as delighted about that as Sutton and Jonathan had been the last time this infamous Cookie Lady put in an appearance.

"Everybody's in the activities room," she told him. "She just started reading not too long ago. If you hurry, you'll get to hear some of the story."

"I think I will," Paul said.

He headed to the center of the U-shaped building. Classrooms and nap rooms ringed the perimeter, but the center of activity was the core of the horseshoe, a large room subdivided by a hundred-gallon aquarium to the right and a bunny cage to the left.

The fish usually caught his eye and gave him a reason to pause. But not today. His gaze zeroed in on the story corner.

What he saw floored him.

Like peacocks showing off their plumes, Amber Montgomery and his daughter strutted around, clucking and fluttering their arms. The children sitting on mats on the floor giggled, some of them rolling over on the floor laughing.

The sight of Amber and Sutton stopped Paul cold for two reasons. Sutton never, ever opened up like that. And the two of them together had to be the most adorable sight he'd seen in a long time.

Chapter Four

After finishing their clucking, Amber and Sutton turned back to the storybook. Amber read a page of the barnyard tale. Sutton, lifting the book high so everyone could see the pictures, spotted him.

"Daddy!"

Amber looked up.

Paul knew the exact moment when Sutton's greeting registered with Amber and she recognized him.

Her eyes shuttered and the light so evident a moment ago disappeared. She swallowed, and he watched as a shudder seemed to move through her. She held his gaze—almost defiantly, Paul decided—then deliberately turned her attention back to the children and the book.

"Hi there, sweetheart," he said to Sutton.

"I'm the helper today."

"Is that a fact?"

Sutton smiled and nodded, her pigtails bobbing. Paul's heart wrenched. It had been so long since he'd seen her animated—or talkative. And the woman who'd made it so was the very one who even now surreptitiously inched away from the girl. But was it really away from Sutton, or was it away from him? Paul was afraid he knew the answer.

Some people just didn't like cops. He needed to apologize to her again, and today was his opportunity. After she passed out the cookies, he'd have a word with her. But Paul watched her withdrawal and wondered what she was hiding—and why he took her rebuff personally.

"Cookie Lady, are you going to finish the story?"

Amber jerked as if she'd been pinched. "I... I... Yes."

She reached for the book Sutton held and tried to see beyond the police chief, who suddenly stood much closer than she liked. She stuck her head in the book, anxious to finish the tale so she could escape. But her skin grew clammy and she lost her grip on the book.

Sutton caught it and glanced at her. "We still have three more pages, Cookie Lady."

Amber gave the girl what she hoped was a smile, then quickly read the remaining pages of the book. She closed it and hopped up while the children applauded. Rubbing her hands against her apron she asked, "Who'd like a cookie now?"

Every child's hand shot straight up. Amber lifted the napkin from the basket and carefully handed the cookie basket to Sutton. "Do you know what to do?"

Sutton nodded. "Everybody gets one cookie. At the end, I get two."

"That's right," Amber said. Taking the little girl's hand in her own, Amber led her to the front row of children eagerly awaiting the treat. Then she excused herself.

"Amber?"

"Miss Montgomery?"

Amber ignored both Marnie and the police chief. She headed straight to the rest room, a place to which she knew he wouldn't follow her.

She closed herself behind a stall and leaned her head against the door.

Breathe, she coached herself. *Breathe.*

Her pulse pounded. She felt as if she'd been dumped into the middle of a marathon.

She tried to convince herself that she was in no physical danger from him, that she'd simply overreacted. But she couldn't get her heartbeat to slow down, or her fear to subside.

A knock on the stall door made her jump. "Who is it?"

"Amber, are you okay?" Marnie asked through the door. "What happened?"

"I'm...fine," she said, a hitch in her voice.

"You don't sound fine," Marnie persisted. "And you looked like you were about to faint out there. Would you like some water?"

"No, thank you."

For several minutes, the only sound in the rest room

was Amber's breathing. Amber's feet hadn't moved from the edge of the door where she stood.

"Amber, are you okay? Come out. Please."

"I will." But she made no move to unlatch the door.

Marnie knocked again. "Amber?"

Amber closed her eyes and tried to remember everything she'd been taught, tried to recall some of the deep-breathing exercises she'd learned.

"Amber, you're scaring me."

She forced herself to face her fear, and slid the lock free.

Marnie reached for her hands and clasped them in her own. "You're freezing."

Amber tried to tug her hands free. "I'm fine. Really. I just..." She shrugged, unable to finish the explanation, sure that Marnie with her perfect life and perfect job wouldn't be able to understand her problem, let alone identify with it.

Marnie pulled Amber toward the sink. She ran cool water and made a compress from paper towels that she then pressed on Amber's forehead. Then she ran warm water and plunged Amber's hands under the steady stream. She rubbed Amber's hands, getting the blood circulating again.

"Does that feel better?"

Amber nodded, and Marnie handed her a paper towel to dry her hands.

"You want to tell me what's going on? You ran out of there like something was on fire."

"Nothing's wrong," Amber said automatically.

If she kept telling herself that, maybe she'd eventually believe it.

For a moment, it seemed as if Marnie would let it go....

"I want you to know I care about you, Amber. You do good work here with the kids. I'd hate to lose you."

"What makes you think I'm going somewhere?"

Marnie stilled her hands and stared at Amber. "I see it in your eyes. You look scared and ready to bolt." Then their gazes connected in the mirror above the sink. "What can I do to help you?"

Amber shook her head. "Nothing."

"I think I know what's wrong."

"I doubt it," Amber said.

"Yes, Amber. You see, it takes one to know one."

"Is the Cookie Lady coming back?"

Paul glanced at one of the aides who'd stepped in after both Amber and Marnie Shepherd disappeared.

"I'm sure she will," he told the child.

"Hey, Chief Evans, can I take a ride in your police car?"

"Maybe next time, Max." He bit back a smile at the boy's excited grin.

"Tomorrow?"

"Maybe not that soon."

"Okay," the boy said, confident that the promise extracted from the police chief would eventually be fulfilled.

Sutton finished passing out the cookies and brought the basket to the front of the Story Corner. She placed her two cookies on a paper napkin, then carefully folded the two cloth napkins, bringing as much care to the job as Amber would have, as she placed them inside the basket. She then put the basket on the table next to Amber's rocker.

"I was the helper today, Daddy."

Paul squatted down and gave her a hug. "And it looks to me like you did a terrific job."

"I get two cookies." She offered him one. "Would you like this one?"

Paul took a bite and munched on it, savoring every bite.

Wow. No wonder Caleb was so opposed to sharing. He glanced in the direction of the rest rooms.

His radio squawked. Paul pressed the speaker button at his shoulder unit. "Go ahead."

"Chief, we've got a domestic in progress on Patterson in East Wayside."

"On the way," Paul answered.

"Daddy, what's a domestic?"

"Domestic disturbance. Right, Chief?" Max piped up. "Somebody's hitting somebody."

Had it been any other kid, Paul would have been disturbed at the child's knowledge. But Max Young came from a long line of law enforcement officers. "Right, Max."

With a final glance toward the place Amber had skittered off to, Paul said farewell to the children and to the aide. He hugged Sutton and placed a hand on Jonathan's shoulder. "I'll see you guys soon, okay?"

Jonathan, who didn't care for public displays of affection, edged closer to Paul. "You'll catch 'em, right?"

"Catch who?"

Jonathan motioned for Paul to get closer. He leaned down and watched the boy look to his right and left. "The domestic disturbance. You'll get the bad man, won't you?"

Paul blinked, sudden moisture in his eyes. He wrapped an arm around his son's shoulders and pulled him close for a hug. "I'll get 'em, Jon."

Marnie peeked out the bathroom door. "He's gone."

"I'm not afraid of him."

"Uh-huh," Marnie said. "That's why we've been in here ten minutes."

"I need to go."

Marnie stopped Amber with a hand on her arm. "Whatever's going on, Amber, I'm here for you and so is the Lord. I'm keeping you in my prayers."

Amber opened her mouth to say something, thought better of it, then slipped from the rest room. Her Cookie Lady persona cloaked around her again, she bid farewell to the children, thanked Sutton for her help and got a huge hug in return.

Startled, Amber didn't quite know what to do. Then she wrapped her arms around the girl, fusing both of them in the much-needed embrace. "You take good care now, okay?"

The little girl nodded. "I love you, Cookie Lady," Sutton whispered in her ear.

Astounded, Amber blinked. When was the last time she'd gotten unconditional love? Swallowing hard, she smiled at the girl, tugged on a pigtail and hightailed it out of Sunshine and Rainbows.

Who knew delivering cookies and reading a story could be just as dangerous to her state of mind as catering a Wayside Revelers' event?

When she got home, two messages awaited her.

She pressed the button on her answering machine, then tucked away the cookie basket and put the aprons in a laundry bin.

"Hi, Amber." Haley's voice rang out. "I was just checking in. I'll try to catch you later. Wanted to ask you something."

"More like checking up on me," Amber said, as the machine beeped and forwarded to the next message.

"It's me again," Haley said. "Can you join us for dinner tonight? Matt's going to grill."

Amber's mouth watered at the thought. She was a whiz in the kitchen, but Matt Brandon-Dumaine worked wonders on a barbecue grill. She could hear his voice in the background. Then Haley laughed on the recorder.

"Matt says to tell you if you come over he might, emphasis on the word *might,* share one of his secret barbecue sauce recipes with you. Steaks and chicken go on the grill at six. Hope you can make it."

Amber smiled. She had to give it to Haley—her cousin

never stopped trying to get her to live a little, to do some socializing in Wayside.

But Amber had no interest in developing any close ties beyond those she needed to make and maintain her catering company. She'd learned the hard way that friends and even family—Haley excepted, of course— couldn't be counted on to be there in a pinch.

Just one person had Amber's best interests at heart: Amber.

She could tolerate having dinner with Haley and Matt or a cup of coffee with Kara Spencer, her longtime friend and sometime therapist. Beyond that, Amber wasn't interested. She couldn't afford to be.

On her arrival at the barbecue, her eyebrows rose as she noted the number of cars in front of Matt and Haley's large house. And the moment she walked into the living room, Amber realized she'd been set up. Not only that, but it was a setup operating on two fronts.

"Hi, Amber!"

Trapped.

Too late to turn and head back out the door.

"Hello, Caleb," Amber greeted. "Funny seeing you here."

She cast her eyes toward her cousin, who merely smiled sweetly as she presented a tray of almost depleted hors d'oeuvres to Cliff Baines, *Reverend* Cliff Baines, pastor of Haley's church.

A single guy and the preacher. Great, Amber thought.

Just great. Maybe instead of eating dessert, they could just get married.

"Why don't you replenish that," Amber suggested, as Haley came around with the tray. "I'll help you," Amber said, lacing her voice with sweetness.

Haley wasn't fooled, though, as she followed Amber into her kitchen.

"You wouldn't hurt a pregnant lady," Haley said, as the swinging door closed behind the two of them. Outside on the deck, under an awning that protected him from the rain starting to fall, Matt waved.

Amber waved at Matt, but glared at her cousin. "I'm deciding," she said. She glanced at Haley's stomach. "You're not even showing yet."

Haley lifted her hands to frame her face. "But Matt says I have a glow."

"You're glowing, all right. This was no spur-of-the-moment cookout, Haley. You know I hate setups."

"What setup? It's just a few friends."

"Uh-huh," Amber said. "Your pastor and his wife to hound me about not going to church, and that puppy-dog-eyed policeman."

"Cliff and Nancy are friends. They aren't going to hound you or anybody else. And I'd hardly call Caleb puppy-dog-eyed."

Amber reached for and munched on a celery stick filled with cream cheese and pimento. "He reminds me of the Ebb character from Classic TV."

Haley shook her head. "You *do* need to get out more.

Satellite TV is addling your brain. And for the record, Caleb is also a friend. You're family. What's wrong with having friends and family over for dinner?"

Amber knew she wouldn't win this round with Haley, but she had a trump card. "When you're eight months pregnant and craving a lemon tart or a honey pecan roll, I'm going to be all sold out."

"That's mean," Haley said, but she laughed.

Matt came in, greeted Amber with a "Hey, cuz" as he leaned in to buss her on the cheek, then carried a bowl of something to the dining room.

Haley moved to follow him. "Come on. Let's get these out to everyone."

The doorbell rang as they reentered the living room.

"I'll get it," Matt said.

A moment later he opened the door to Paul Evans and Marnie Shepherd.

Amber saw the pair and let out a shaky breath. Is that what Marnie had meant in the rest room at Sunshine and Rainbows? That Amber didn't have to fear Paul because Marnie knew him to be an honorable man. *Her* man? They'd never really talked about personal stuff, so Amber had no way of knowing whether Marnie was seeing the police chief.

"Did you make these?" Caleb asked.

"Huh?"

Amber took her eyes off the pair at the door, turning her attention to Caleb, who was enjoying a corn fritter. "No. Haley did. Or maybe Matt."

"They're probably not as good as yours."

Amber looked at Caleb as if seeing him for the first time. "Excuse me." She fled to the kitchen.

Caleb looked from her retreating back to his boss at the front door.

"He followed me home, can I keep him?" Marnie said with a smile, indicating the police chief.

"Come on in," Matt invited.

She knew it was a little crazy but Amber had to talk to someone right now. From the wall phone in the kitchen, she called Kara—and got an answering machine.

She slammed the phone down, then tried a little deep breathing. If she kept jumping at shadows like this she'd be a basket case, not to mention right back where she'd been three years ago when she first came home to Wayside.

Leaning against the sink, she considered her options. She could escape out the sliding glass doors and go home, or she could face her fears and walk out into that living room.

The choice, to some degree, was taken away from her when the kitchen door swung open and in walked Wayside, Oregon's Police Chief Paul Evans.

Amber gripped the edge of the sink behind her. She assessed all of him. Tonight he didn't wear the uniform that marked him as an officer of the law. Gone also were the gun, club and cuffs. He stood at the door in jeans, work

boots and a chambray shirt. He looked more like a cow-
boy than a cop.

He's just a man, Amber coached herself. *You're in a safe
place. He's just a man.*

"Hello, Miss Montgomery. I waited at the day care the
other day to have a word with you, but I got a call and
had to leave."

She didn't say anything.

He took three steps forward. Amber forced herself
not to flinch.

He must have noticed something because his eyes narrowed a bit, and the smile on his mouth fell a notch, not
enough that any casual observer would even notice. But
Amber wasn't a casual observer. Fight-or-flight kicked in.
Since he now blocked both exits, it would have to be
fight.

"I don't see how that concerns me." She deliberately
aimed for belligerent and defensive.

"I want to apologize," he said, glancing at her arm.
"About the other night. I didn't mean to grab you or to
leave a bruise."

"The complaint letters are already mailed." That
wasn't true, but he didn't have to know it.

"I mistook you for one of the Revelers."

"So I look seventy years old?"

A smile tilted the corners of his mouth and a dimple
showed. "Hardly, Miss Montgomery."

She told herself she wasn't going to be charmed by
that smile, that her guard would remain up. But she did

allow her body to loosen. She'd been holding herself so erect that she'd need a masseuse to get the knots out.

"Please let me finish. I also want to thank you for something," he said.

"Thank me? For what?"

"For bringing a smile again to my daughter's face."

❧ Chapter Five ❧

"She's a sweet girl."

"But she's been through a lot. It's not very often I see her smile and giggle and act like the five-year-old she is."

"What's wrong with her?" The question was out before the impertinence of it dawned on Amber. She'd always been one to speak her mind first and worry about the consequences later. The cloud that shadowed his face told her without words that she'd done it again. "Never mind," she added. "Don't answer that. Your apology's accepted, Chief Evans. Now, if you'll excuse me."

She gave him a wide berth as she moved toward the door leading back to the living room and the safety and comfort of other people.

Paul watched her retreat. He didn't feel a need to bolster his own defense mechanisms in response to her anger; to his utter amazement, what he was feeling was a surge of protectiveness. But everything about Amber Montgomery said "woman with a past—avoid like the plague."

He couldn't determine if she didn't like cops in general or if it was him in particular. Whatever the case, Amber brought out in him an interest that extended beyond the professional.

Since it clearly wasn't reciprocated, he'd have to move on.

He hadn't believed anyone existed who could draw the kids out of the shells in which they'd lived these past few years. But Amber Montgomery, the Cookie Lady, had done just that, not only for Sutton and Jonathan, but for him, as well.

Moving to Oregon, this little town in particular, had facilitated the healing process for the three of them. Paul hadn't expected to find love in Wayside. But he'd hoped to find a woman with whom he was compatible, someone who could open her heart and accept not only him, but the two children he was now raising as his own.

Meanwhile, as another consideration, Marnie Shepherd was great with the kids. They liked her and the time they spent at Sunshine and Rainbows. Of course, no one would ever replace their mother, but Jonathan and Sutton still needed mothering. Every child did.

"Come on out here, Chief. The reverend is going to say grace, then we'll eat."

Paul joined the others in the living room where Cliff Baines waited to lead the dinner guests in prayer.

Looking around the assembled group, Paul realized just what Haley and Matt Brandon-Dumaine were up to. Their little soiree included two married couples and four singles who looked likely to be matched up. And if the episode with the cookies in the squad car served as an indicator, Caleb was well and truly infatuated with Amber Montgomery.

That meant Matt and Haley had paired him with Marnie for the evening. Paul wasn't opposed to that. He enjoyed speaking with her at church. With her pretty smile, bubbly personality and her way with children, Marnie was an attractive woman. He'd never believed in love at first sight or any of that romantic nonsense. People got together because they were compatible. And Marnie got along well with Jonathan and Sutton. That was a good place to begin.

He moved into the small circle they'd formed for grace and looked at Marnie again. She smiled as she leaned over, telling Haley something. Paul nodded to himself, silently agreeing with the not-so-subtle matchmaking.

Maybe he would ask Marnie out to dinner and a movie. For some reason, though, Paul's eye kept wandering to the aloof blonde with the haunted eyes. On the pretense of moving a chair, he shifted his position toward her.

Amber had been standing next to Matt, but when she bowed her head, a strong hand clasped hers. Her gaze flew to her right. Paul Evans stood there, tall, strong, his head bowed in prayer, his hand holding hers. Warmth suffused her.

She cleared her throat and tried to ease her hand from his. But he held on as the minister started to pray.

"Thank you, Lord, for bringing good friends together to share good times and good food. Amen."

Amber opened one eye to peer at Cliff. That was it? That was his idea of grace? What about blessing the hands that prepared the meal, and three minutes of other supplications and prayer-time clichés? She knew them all.

"Amber?"

She glanced up at Paul. "Yes?" she said, surprised that he didn't know you weren't supposed to talk during a prayer or moment of silence.

"You can let my hand go now."

Her gaze swept the room. The others, already having broken away from the prayer circle, headed toward the dining room. Amber's face flamed. She dropped Paul's hand and hastened a safe distance away.

"Steaks are ready!" Matt called out from the kitchen before she could think of a good reason to leave the dinner party.

Rain may have chased the cookout indoors, but it didn't dampen the enthusiasm inside. Since the evening was supposed to be informal, everyone grabbed a plate and helped themselves from the feast Matt had laid out on the dining room table. Instead of settling there, Haley led the way back to the living room, where the guests spread out wherever they felt comfortable.

For Nancy Baines and Marnie, that meant the floor with the coffee table pressed into service.

Caleb perched on the edge of a chair near them. "I'll grab some napkins for you ladies."

When Paul and Cliff claimed two of the TV trays, Amber moved hers a bit away.

Matt got his wife situated and kissed her.

"Hey, none of that," Amber said.

"Yeah," Marnie added, laughing. "You'll make the rest of us jealous."

"I still have six months to go, but he acts as if delivery is imminent."

"It is," Matt said. "The time's going to fly by."

While Marnie and Nancy asked about baby names and nursery colors, Amber watched the byplay between Haley and Matt. A lot of love flowed between them. In their soft gazes swelling with shared affection and regard it was there for all the world to see.

Once upon a time she'd loved like that—or so she'd thought at the time. The love hadn't flowed both ways, though, and Amber found out the hard way just how much she'd pay for that.

She supposed that some people truly were happy. But for her, love was a lie she'd learned to reject. She'd learned to simply live, day to day. And that suited her just fine.

Again and again, however, her gaze slipped to her cousin, and something akin to jealousy snipped at her, surprising her.

Keep it light, she coached herself. If she allowed what-if thoughts to intrude, she'd never make it through the evening.

For a few minutes, the four couples ate in companionable silence, the only accompaniment to their meal an instrumental CD playing in the background.

"I've got to hand it to you, Matt," Caleb said. "You have grilling skills."

"He's supposed to reveal the sauce recipe," Amber said. "The promise of that is the only thing that lured me here tonight."

"Ah," Caleb said. "And here I thought it was the thrill of seeing me again."

"In your dreams, Jenkins," she said.

Caleb chuckled at that.

This she could handle, keeping it casual. The easy camaraderie in the room masked the awkwardness Amber felt around Paul.

Over a glass of cider, she studied the police chief. Without the uniform, he didn't look nearly as intimidating as he had previously. Of course, he was still tall and broad-shouldered, but that made him look solid, the sort you could depend on in a crisis.

Like Kyle.

His gaze connected with hers. Caught staring, Amber blushed and averted her eyes. She cut a piece of steak, making careful work of slicing the meat just so. When she dared, she glanced up.

He was still looking at her. He smiled.

Amber's pulse rate leaped.

"Anyone want more potatoes?" She hopped up from her seat.

"I do," Paul said. "I'll help you."

"I'm closest," Marnie said. "Sit down, both of you."

Before either could object, Marnie disappeared and came back from the dining room with a tray of skewered roasted potatoes with red and green bell peppers. She offered the tray to everyone, sending—at least it seemed so to Amber—a brighter, longer smile in Chief Evans's direction.

"So, what's going on over at Community Christian these days?" Caleb asked.

"Camp. Camp and more camp," Nancy said. "Forty-five kids this year. We have a good crop of seniors who've been with us and will serve as the teen counselors, but still I worry."

"Don't mind my wife," Cliff said. "She's the overall coordinator of our annual fall jamboree and things are just a little stressful right now."

"That's because it's less than a week away, and I still have two weeks' worth of work to do."

Cliff placed a hand on her shoulder as he passed by with a refill from the dining room. "It all comes together beautifully each year. This year won't be an exception."

"We're really blessed to have so many volunteers," Haley said. "Everyone from the church pitches in and helps in some way. And with that community grant Kara got for us this year, we're able to do a lot more."

Amber let the conversation flow around her. She had nothing to say and wondered just how soon she could make her escape without seeming too obvious.

If, for some silly reason, she felt another nip or two from the green-eyed monster as she looked at Matt and Haley, and even at Cliff and Nancy Baines, the preacher and his wife, she let it slide. They looked so...happy.

It didn't matter. She didn't go to Community Christian or any other church—and had no intention of starting anytime soon. Plus, through the years she'd had enough church camp to last her not one or two, but several lifetimes.

Amber couldn't remember the last time she could count herself truly happy. And she now knew she'd never really been in love. Not the way the Baineses were in love. She'd been part of a couple once. And all she had to say for the experience was good riddance.

"So, how are you finding Wayside?"

The question, directed to Paul from Nancy Baines, made Amber look up from her plate.

Paul swallowed a bite of food. "Just fine, Mrs. Baines. It's a lot different from L.A."

Amber's throat constricted. "You're from Los Angeles?"

He nodded. "I needed to get Sutton and Jon out of the big city environment." He shook his head. "It wasn't healthy for any of us. And, where I lived and how I used to work didn't lend itself to fatherhood. At least, not the way they needed."

"The children are just adorable," Nancy said. "I have Sutton in my Sunday school class."

"Yes, she really enjoys that," Paul said. "I'm glad I found Community Christian. That was one thing I thought I might miss about Los Angeles. Even though I worked crazy hours, I had a church family that was devoted to the gospel and family values, both incongruous notions in L.A."

Caleb helped himself to another kabob. "The chief here was on the LAPD for—what?—about twelve years, right Chief?"

Amber gasped. Her eyes widened and her fork clattered to her plate. She stood up so fast she almost lost her balance. "Excuse me." And she left the room.

Matt and Haley shared a look.

Cliff put his plate down. "Maybe I should…"

Haley got up. "She'll be all right. I'll go check on her," she said as she headed toward the kitchen.

"Was it something I said?" Paul asked.

"Uh, don't worry about it. I'm sure it's just something to do with setting out dessert," Matt said, but his look was hardly reassuring.

Spending an evening with a room full of church people, even ones she knew, wasn't Amber's idea of a great time, but she'd found herself laughing at the byplay among Cliff, Nancy Baines, and even Caleb, and actually enjoying herself…until just now.

He was one of *them*.

"Amber, are you all right?"

She shook her head. "I have to leave."

Haley wrapped an arm around her cousin's shoulders. "I know. I'm sorry, Amber. I didn't realize he was—"

"It's not your fault." Amber stopped her. "This is my bugaboo. I have to learn to live with it."

Amber headed to the sliding glass doors that led to the deck and yard of Matt and Haley's home.

"It's still raining outside," Haley said. "Let me get you an umbrella."

"I'll be fine. Sorry to break up your party."

And then she escaped into the dark night—a night a lot like one she'd tried for a long time to banish from her memory.

"I think tonight was supposed to be a setup," Marnie told Caleb Jenkins later.

He laughed. "So it wasn't just me getting that vibe."

"I think now that she's happily married and starting a family, Haley has decided to play town matchmaker."

Caleb held the door for Marnie, who'd been dropped off at Haley and Matt's by a co-worker.

"The thing I'm trying to figure out," he said, "is who was supposed to be with whom."

"I think I was supposed to be with Chief Evans. Did you see that pleased look on Haley's face when I appeared at the door with him?"

"How did that come about? Happenstance?"

She waited until he came around and settled behind the wheel. "Something like that. He drove up at the same time I was dashing through the rain for the front door.

So if Haley planned for me to get cozy with Chief Evans, that means she has her eye on you and Amber as a pair."

"Amber is a friend."

Marnie smiled. "Mm-hmm."

Caleb started the car. "Have you ever thought about selling the house?"

She gave him a knowing look, but didn't call him on the abrupt change of subject. "Yes." The single word came out slow and long. Marnie shifted in her seat.

He glanced at her, but didn't follow up with the next obvious question.

"It's a lot of house," she said. "Selling it makes sense."

Caleb nodded, but not because he agreed with her or particularly liked the direction of the conversation and what selling that house might mean. It just seemed the right thing to do at the moment. But instead of following that thread of their touch-and-go conversation, he asked another question that had been on his mind for a while.

"So, how have you been? Really been, I mean?"

Marnie chuckled softly, relieving the sudden tension in the car. The history between them didn't get discussed very often. "I'll answer that if you admit you have a secret thing for Amber Montgomery."

Caleb raised an eyebrow. He knew that to deny it again would be protesting too much.

So they drove the rest of the way to her home in silence.

Caleb didn't regret asking the question about how she

was really doing. He still wanted an answer, but maybe it was still too soon for her. Maybe it would never be the right time. He worried about Marnie. On the outside, everything looked okay, but they never talked about the thing that stood between them—the element that connected them. By not talking about Roy, they could pretend everything was just fine.

He pulled into the driveway, careful to skirt the thick tree trunk that pushed through the gravel. He knew Marnie would rather cut off one of her own limbs than cut the tree down, so at some point the driveway would have to be realigned and rerouted around the ancient oak, the only non-maple tree on Maple Street.

He came around and opened the passenger-side door, an old-fashioned habit he'd been taught as a child. Some women liked it, others made fun of him for doing it. Marnie, he knew, was in the first group.

"For the record," he said as if they'd never stopped talking, "Amber bakes a mean cookie, but I don't have a thing for her. And anyway, she's not interested."

Marnie opened her mouth to say something, then apparently changed her mind. "Thanks for the ride, Caleb."

He nodded. "Anytime."

He meant it, too, but didn't know how to go further—to say the important things that stood between them.

So he saw her to the door and waited until she let herself into the house. She turned in the doorway, looking soft and vulnerable and painfully beautiful.

"Do you want to come in for a cup of coffee?"

Yes.

But he knew the way he was feeling right now, it was best if he went on his way. "No, it's kind of late. I'll just head on home."

She hesitated. "All right, then. You take care. Thanks for the lift." She turned to go, then paused. "Caleb?"

"Yes?"

She raised a hand and stepped forward. "I... I just thought you could use a hug."

Caleb closed his eyes.

No. No. No. *Yes.*

She wrapped her arms around him and hugged him close. Caleb stored up every moment of the brief embrace.

"Thanks again for giving me a lift. And, Caleb, if you like her, you should tell her. Amber's a nice girl. You take care, okay?"

When he nodded, she waved from the door and then closed it.

Caleb Jenkins stood there for a while, watching lights go on as Marnie made her way through her home, a big house made for the family she very much deserved but didn't have.

Marnie had always been a special woman, blessed with a gift for making people feel exceptional, wanted, loved. That's why she was such an asset to Sunshine and Rainbows. The children blossomed under her care.

There were so many things he wanted to say to her. He wished he could explain. To open up with her the way he'd always wanted to. But he didn't have the right—had never had the right to hope for anything more than polite friendliness with Marnie. Especially now.

Making light of his social life, or lack thereof, came easy to Caleb. He dated now and then, and flirted with a few women like Amber just to keep the loneliness at bay, but nothing serious.

How *could* he get serious about any other woman? His heart had always belonged to Marnie Shepherd—his brother's wife.

❧ Chapter Six ❧

Hours later, Amber pulled into the drive and parked behind Kara's car. Even though Kara was engaged to a multi-millionaire, recording artist Marcus Ambrose, she still drove the same car she always had. A For Sale sign in the front yard was the only indication that any change was in the works in her life. Soon Kara would move to a new home outside Los Angeles.

Just the name of the city brought a shudder.

She didn't have many friends and the thought of losing one of them hurt, particularly since visits to L.A. were completely out of the question. The City of Angels might be large, but not large enough for Amber to escape the memories of her years there. When she'd left, she'd vowed never to set foot there again.

She glanced up at the second-floor windows. Dark. Maybe she should have called first.

But before she chickened out, Amber went to the back door and rang the bell. Then she leaned on it.

A few moments later, a light flicked on in the kitchen. "Who's there?"

"It's me, Kara. Amber."

The back porch light clicked on, bathing Amber in its glow. Then she heard the dead bolt slide.

To her credit, Kara didn't exclaim about the lateness of the hour or ask why Amber was standing on her porch in the rain. She just opened her arms and let the troubled woman in.

Fifteen minutes later, dried off and with a cup of chamomile tea to warm her inside and out, Amber sat in one of the comfy chairs in Kara's sunroom.

"Do you want to talk about it?"

Amber stared into her mug for a bit, then she blinked back tears. "You've been very patient with me."

Kara, a psychologist by profession—though she primarily did community block grant work these days—never balked when Amber showed up at her door, a honey pecan roll in hand and things on her mind. Kara knew some of what had happened to Amber in L.A., but Amber had never told anyone—not even Haley—the whole story.

"I thought it was all behind me," she said. "But it's back again and I don't know what to do."

"What's back, Amber?"

"It's like a hole inside me, a hole that's eating away at my insides. It was all patched up and doing okay.

None of the bad stuff was leaking out. Then he showed up."

"Wait, what? Who is 'he'?"

"The cop."

Kara tread carefully here. "Your former boyfriend?"

Amber lifted wide hollow eyes to her friend. Trust didn't come easily, but Kara had proven herself to be a friend, someone who could be relied on.

"It's the police chief," Amber finally said. "Chief Evans."

Though she tried to hide it, Kara's surprise came through in her voice. "Chief Evans hurt you?"

Amber shook her head. "No. Not in the way you mean."

Kara leaned back in her chair, waiting for Amber to gather her thoughts and open up. This time, Kara instinctively knew, Amber wouldn't run when the memories and the pain closed in. She could see it in the other woman's eyes—the determination to move on, to heal.

To face the monster from her past.

Paul spent a frustrating couple of days trying to figure out just what was with Amber Montgomery. Everything he said, every move he made, seemed to spook her. She responded to him as if she were guilty of a crime still undiscovered.

Paul considered himself a pretty good judge of character, yet all of his instincts went on alert around Amber. His first thought was to run her name through NCIC. The

National Crime Information Center had data on every known and wanted criminal. Amber didn't look like a criminal, but fugitives from the law came in all shapes and sizes.

The only problem with his instincts when it came to this particular woman was that for the first time in his law enforcement career, he found himself having a difficult time ascertaining if the gut feeling that had never let him down before was professional or personal. Amber intrigued him, mainly because she evoked in him so many conflicting emotions: wariness, desire, the urge to protect, the need to unravel her mysteries.

And that's the part that the cop in him wouldn't let go. Wayside, Oregon, his new home, the place he'd sworn to protect and serve, was just the sort of town that would make a good hideout for someone who wanted to disappear. Its population of 17,800—well, now with him and the kids, 17,803—was just big enough for newcomers to blend in if they didn't make any waves, and just small enough to provide a sense of comfort. That's why *he'd* chosen it. And the good Lord knew he'd needed a place to be renewed.

Amber Montgomery was an enigma. A well-protected enigma. He'd tried to find out from his hosts, Matt and Haley Brandon-Dumaine, just what had been said or done that spooked Amber. They'd been polite, but close-mouthed. Ditto for Pastor Cliff.

Paul had another source available to him, though.

Caleb liked Amber, which meant he could probably answer some questions.

Even though Wayside was small-town America at its best, the community never missed out on any federal money that the police bureau knew of. So in addition to the state-of-the-art headquarters building, the Wayside Police Bureau boasted not one, but two community policing branches, one of which was in East Wayside, a particularly crime-ridden area. He convinced himself it was a public safety issue and not a personal concern that made him corner his patrol chief near the command desk at the police station.

"What's up with Amber Montgomery?"

Caleb grinned. "I wondered how long it would take you to ask."

Paul narrowed his eyes, but Caleb held up a hand to stave off the potential irritation.

"Before I answer, I need to know who's asking. Paul the man who is my friend, or Police Chief Evans, my boss?"

In his few months in Wayside, Paul had made a few friends. He counted Caleb Jenkins among them. He didn't, however, want to admit that he found himself attracted to Amber. "The police chief."

Caleb folded his arms across his chest. "Really? Well, in that case, *Chief* Evans, Ms. Montgomery is one of our upstanding citizens, a small-business owner."

With a jerk of his head, Paul steered Caleb away from listening ears. They walked a few feet to a snack-machine area. "All right, *I* want to know. What did I say that sent her flying out the door the other night?"

"I don't know."

Paul's patience, already frayed, didn't improve with that answer. "What do you mean, you don't know?"

Caleb shrugged. "I don't know. Honest. I met Amber a few years ago. She'd enrolled in a self-defense class I was teaching over at the college. You should have seen her then, Chief. Hollow-eyed. She was incredibly thin. She looked like a refugee from a war zone."

Something crossed Caleb's face then. "I—" He shrugged again. "I felt responsible somehow, even though I'd just met her. I wanted to protect her, keep her safe."

Paul could identify with that. He felt the same—unreasonable—way about her. Though he'd never admit as much to his patrol sergeant. Maybe there was nothing extraordinary about Amber except that the fragile blonde brought out the protectiveness trait in some men. The Amber he'd met bore no resemblance to the hollow-eyed woman Caleb described. Paul's Amber was vibrant, active, and great with kids. His kids.

"She started baking one day," Caleb said. "She made some honey pecan rolls for a booth during Wayside Market Days. They sold out in no time. Then someone, probably Haley, talked her into preparing a basket for the picnic basket auction."

"Picnic basket auction?"

Caleb quickly explained about the annual event that

was a part of Wayside Market Days. "Amber always makes up a lunch basket filled with good stuff that goes for a pretty penny during a public auction over at the gazebo. But Matt Brandon-Dumaine holds the record for the most money bid on a single basket. Haley's, of course."

"And what does this have to do with anything?"

"You wanted to know about Amber, so I'm telling you," Caleb said. "You do want a complete snapshot. Right?"

When Paul nodded, Caleb continued. "Everybody likes her—those honey pecan rolls of hers transcended her privateness. They were the beginning of her relationship with Wayside. She's responsible for a lot of memberships at the gym."

"Because she has a bakery shop near the gym?"

Caleb chuckled. "Nope. Because folks have to work off the pounds that creep up as a result of too many of Amber's honey pecan rolls."

"I'm going to have to get one of those things," Paul muttered.

"Thanks for agreeing to do this," Marnie told Amber on Wednesday. Along with one of the Sunshine and Rainbows assistants, they'd set up the cooking demonstration area. Big plastic mixing bowls and wooden spoons were at the ready, along with measuring utensils and ingredients just waiting for little hands to create yummy masterpieces. "The kids are so excited."

Amber looked around. "Where is everybody?"

"In their classrooms. Since they're going to be so keyed up with you here, we thought a quiet period beforehand made sense."

Twenty minutes later, the center room bustled with kids, parent volunteers, and Amber, who was in her element.

"What's the first thing you should do before you start cooking?" she asked the kids.

"Wash your hands!" several of them yelled.

"That's right. Who remembered to do that?"

"I did, Cookie Lady."

Amber looked at the soft-spoken girl in the front row. Her brother and two other girls were her table partners. "Good job, Sutton," Amber said.

She was grateful that their father hadn't put in an appearance. Marnie said he'd been delayed. That was fine by Amber. With any luck, they'd be finished by the time he completed his police duties. The three other parent volunteers and one of the center's assistants could easily handle the job of monitoring the children's progress.

Over the next ten minutes, she taught the children about measuring dry ingredients. The no-bake cookies included oatmeal, chocolate chips, crisped rice cereal and mini chocolate candies. The sugar high alone would keep them all bouncing off the walls for a while.

Amber walked along the rows of tables that had been converted into kitchen workstations. She paused at the back of the room to show a girl how to use her spoon to level off a cup of oatmeal.

"Is this too much?" Max Young asked as he dumped half of a five-pound bag of flour into his bowl. White powder poofed up. Max waved his arms, trying vainly to lessen the damage.

"Just a little," Amber said.

She reached for a towel to clean up some of the mess, Max helping. And her hand connected with a much larger, warmer one.

Tingles shot up her spine. She knew who it was without even turning around.

Paul chuckled. "I think that's way more than you need, Max."

"Hi, Chief Evans!" exclaimed Max.

"Hi, Max. Hello, Amber."

"Good afternoon, Chief Evans."

"Please, call me Paul."

Amber was saved from having to agree to that when one of the other parents asked a question. "I'll be right there," she called. "Excuse me," she said to Paul.

Marnie stood watching the parry and retreat between Amber and Paul. She doubted they even realized what was happening between them, all darting eyes and uneasy contact. From her vantage point, they presented an intriguing pair. But, Marnie knew, Amber had a lot to overcome before she'd allow herself to trust a man like Paul Evans.

It wasn't Paul. He had a lot going for him. Plus, he looked like a walking dream. About six feet tall, he had the lean look of a tennis player, and the muscle tone of a man who regularly worked out. In the dictionary next to the entry "all-American boy next door" would be a picture of Paul Evans, his blue eyes sparkling.

Marnie realized her brother-in-law also fit that general description. Sometimes it amazed Marnie that Caleb and his brother Roy had actually come from the same womb. They were different in every way. If she'd met Caleb before meeting Roy...

She smiled, self-deprecating. That didn't even warrant a completed thought. She'd made her choices and there was no going backward hollering, *"I changed my mind. I want Bachelor Number Two."*

Shuddering through the thin turtleneck and pullover sweater, she rubbed her upper arms. She took a deep, calming breath and focused on the children. If she were even remotely interested in another relationship, Marnie might consider Paul. But right now, all she wanted to do was enjoy her hard-won freedom.

Her gaze slid to Amber, who now knelt at a child's side. Marnie knew Amber had been sent into her life for a reason. Marnie could make a pretty educated guess as to why. With the exception of one thing, nothing remarkable had ever happened to Marnie. Amber, Sunshine and Rainbows' beloved Cookie Lady, had been in her prayers for a while and Marnie was in the right place to reach out to her.

"Hi, Daddy!"

"Hey there, pumpkin," Paul said. He swung the girl up for a hug. "Did you make some good cookies?"

Sutton nodded. "But they're not as good as the Cookie Lady's."

He put her down, and reached for one of the brown blobs on her sheet of waxed paper and sampled it. "I disagree," he said. "Yours are way better."

Sutton beamed at him, and then sent a smile Amber's way.

Amber returned the smile, then bent to help another child.

Amber did her best to avoid Paul for the remainder of the kids' cooking class. He put her nerves on edge in ways she didn't want to consider. So instead, she focused on the kids and their questions, and found herself inordinately relieved when the whole thing ended and Paul Evans left, promising to pick up his children at their appointed departure time.

Having finished the last no-bake cookie, the kids thanked Amber and headed back to their classrooms. Amber helped Marnie with the cleanup, then the two women sat in Marnie's office.

"That was fun."

"Yeah," Amber said. "It was." She looked at the day care director. Amber's circle of friends was small, very small—like, all of two—Haley and Kara. Maybe if she put forth a little effort she could turn a close acquaintance into a friend. Marnie seemed like a good bet. And she'd said something that had been nagging at Amber for days now.

"Can I ask you something?"

Marnie leaned back, closed her eyes and rolled the kinks out of her shoulders. "Sure. What's up?"

"The other day when we were talking in the bathroom here, you said 'it takes one to know one.' What did you mean by that?"

Marnie slowly sat up. "You were so upset that day, I didn't think you even heard me." She looked intently at Amber, apparently weighing her words. "We all have secrets, Amber. Some are best kept locked up tight. Others need the light of day to break their bonds."

Trying to keep it light, Amber waggled her brows and lowered her voice to mimic a television announcer's. "What deep, dark secrets could she be hiding?"

Marnie smiled, but she wasn't going to let Amber off, not on something this important. Not when her own spirit was crying out to her that this woman needed her. She said a silent prayer, asking how to say what needed to be said at this particular moment.

"I have scars, Amber. Physical ones that will be with me for a long time, maybe forever. And I have emotional ones. Those, however, I've worked to banish."

Amber scuffed her sneaker on the floor. "What are you talking about?"

Marnie reached a hand out and clasped Amber's. "I think you know."

Pulling away, Amber rose. "I think I don't want to talk about this."

"Amber, being a battered or abused woman is nothing to be ashamed of. That's in your past."

"Who said I was battered?"

"Just a guess," Marnie said with a sad smile. She stood. "Like I said, it takes one to know one, Amber."

The next morning, Eunice Gallagher, known as Mrs. G around Community Christian, greeted Haley and Kara with a smile, glasses of fresh-squeezed orange juice and bad news.

"We have a slight problem."

"So what else is new?" Kara asked. "Let me guess, Sunday school?"

"Thanks," Haley said on a dry note. Since Haley directed the church's Christian education department, any problems in the Sunday school would fall under her purview.

"Nope," Eunice said. "It's not the Sunday school. Or the choir. Or Reverend Baines or the church board."

Kara and Haley exchanged a look. At this time of year, just one big project loomed. "Please tell us it's not the camp."

Eunice winced. "It's the camp."

The two younger women groaned, then headed to the conference room.

"If it's any consolation," Eunice told them, "I called and ordered some honey pecan rolls to help you mull over possible solutions."

Kara pulled out the box containing the student registrations. Every September, Community Christian sponsored a jamboree for the church's youth. This year, however, with Haley's outreach vision in play and Kara's grant-proposal writing skills at work, the camp was being expanded to include fifteen at-risk youth from the community. Several older and experienced teens from Community Christian, including Adam Richardson and Cindy Worthington, would serve as counselors.

Everything was in place for the three-day, two-night camp—from food to activities to adult volunteers. The setup would begin tomorrow night.

"This can't be good," Haley said. "If she has to butter us up with Amber's rolls."

"I was just thinking the same thing," Kara said as she pulled out a chair and sat.

"Okay. We're ready now," Kara said, squeezing her eyes shut really tight. "Tell us the bad news."

Eunice laughed. "It's not *that* bad."

Kara peeked out of one eye. "Really?"

Eunice nodded.

The other two women breathed a sigh of relief and Haley sat down as well. "So all we have to oversee now is loading equipment tomorrow. The kids will start to arrive after four o'clock Friday."

"Well, there's equipment and...one more thing."

Haley and Kara, best friends, shared another look, then each closed one eye and peered at Eunice through the open one.

"Okay. Spill it, Eunice."

"Jocelyn can't come. Her mother is sick down in Salem, and she had to leave."

For a minute, the import didn't sink in. Then Haley and Kara gasped simultaneously.

"What are we going to do with forty-five kids and no cook for three days? Camp starts the day after tomorrow. Jocelyn was supposed to spend tomorrow setting up everything in the kitchen—"

"Yoo-hoo, anybody here?"

"We're back this way, Amber," Eunice called. She got up to greet the chef with the sweet treats.

Haley and Kara turned as Amber appeared in the door, a white baker's box in one hand.

"Amber," they said in silky sweet unison.

Amber eyed them. "Whatever the two of you are thinking, the answer is no."

"Cousin." Haley came around and greeted her. "So nice to see you." She took the box from Amber's hand and placed it on the table. "We've got a wonderful opportunity for you that would also be a tremendous favor to us." They proceeded to explain.

"No," Amber said a few minutes later. "Absolutely not."

"But it's just for a few days."

"Appetizers & More is a gourmet catering company," Amber said. "And despite the fiasco that was the Revelers' dinner dance, I haven't sunk to beans and franks and s'mores, or bug juice."

"What's bug juice?" Eunice asked.

"That icky-sweet orange drink that is a staple at church camps. It draws bugs. Ants and gnats and who knows what else. They always end up in the drinks."

Eunice frowned. "That's nasty. Thankfully we don't serve orange drink at Camp Spirit Fire."

"Please, Amber, we need you," Kara implored. "We're desperate."

Amber eyed them. "How desperate?"

As it turned out, quite so. To pinch-hit, Haley and Kara offered Amber double the rate the camp cook was going to get. Knowing they were on a tight budget and would never agree to it, Amber asked for triple. She smiled smugly at the women's stricken expressions.

Haley and Kara glanced at each other, then, as one, turned to Amber. "Deal."

Chapter Seven

"Deal? What do you mean 'deal'?" She'd been so sure they'd never agree to that much money.

"We'll pay you triple rate," Haley said, restating the deal. "It's fairly easy money for just four days. You'll have some free time to do whatever you'd like. And you'll even have an assistant or two." She nudged Kara, who flipped through a page on top of the registration forms.

Kara ran a manicured finger down a list. "Two assistants," Kara confirmed. "Leanne and Kirsten. They're both very dependable."

She *could* use the money. But that wasn't at all the issue. Amber had had her fill of religious campsites with know-it-all holier-than-thou's. When she'd left home years ago, the one thing she'd promised herself was that she'd never set foot in a mission site again, particularly ones in remote corners of the globe.

"I don't like church camp," she said.

"You won't be attending," Kara said. "Just cooking the meals for the campers."

"I don't like being out in the woods."

"Great!" Haley said a bit too cheerfully. "Camp Spirit Fire is on a private lake. And there are some dorms. You don't even have to go into the woods if you don't want to."

Amber groaned. "I really don't want to do this."

"Please," Haley said. "It's not at all like you think."

"Pretty please," Kara added. "We're desperate."

Eunice rose. "As much as I'd like to listen to the rest of this begging session, I do have some work to do," the church clerk said. "I'll be in my office. Tell me how this all works out."

"Draw up a contract for Amber," Haley called to Eunice's back.

"If I do this, you guys are gonna owe me big," said Amber.

"We're paying you triple scale!" Haley said.

"That's business," Amber said. "This is personal."

"Okay, we'll owe you one," Kara said.

"Two," Amber countered.

"All right," Kara said. "We'll both owe you a big favor."

"And I plan to collect on it," Amber said. She turned to her cousin. "You *know* I really despise church camp."

"This is nothing like that," Haley said. "I promise."

"Humph," Amber said as she stomped out of the conference room muttering, "I knew I shouldn't have agreed to bring an order over here."

"So she's going to do it?" Kara asked.

Sure that once her cousin committed to a deal she'd follow through, Haley nodded. "She'll do it," Haley said with confidence. Then she bit her nail, thinking about Amber's aversion to church, its rituals and its members in general. "Well," she amended, not quite so certain anymore. "I *hope* she'll do it."

"What's the deal with her and church camp?"

"Well, you know my aunt and uncle were missionaries?"

Kara nodded.

"They spent a lot of time in developing countries," Haley said. "Mostly in Central America, primarily Guatemala and Honduras. I think church camp reminds Amber of all those places she and Kyle grew up in. I got to visit with them once before her parents retired from missionary work. I loved it, but Amber hated it. A lot. She wanted a normal life, regular parents."

"Hated it enough to renege on our deal after she thinks about it?"

Haley nodded. "'Fraid so."

"Well, Camp Spirit Fire is hardly the same as a Central American jungle."

"That's not what has me worried."

"What, then?"

Haley pulled out the registrations and pointed to two names: Jonathan and Sutton Evans. "Has she talked to you at all about him?" She left the who of the him unsaid. They were both well aware of Amber's aversion to police officers.

"A little, but..."

"I know, client confidentiality and all that. I'm just worried about her."

"Amber is a friend, not a client," Kara said.

"If she'd just talk about what happened to her in L.A. I think she'd be able to move on."

"What she went through isn't something a person can easily move on from. It takes time."

Haley tapped the registration form for Paul's children. "I just worry that her run-in with Chief Evans at the Revelers' has begun to bring everything back out in the open."

By the time she got to the campsite, Amber knew she should have stuck to her guns. Driving through a rustic gate welcoming people to Community Christian Church's Camp Spirit Fire, Amber's thoughts roamed back through the years to a similar sign over a similar camp.

It had taken two days by a camp truck on an almost nonexistent road and then a five-mile hike to get to the site the Montgomery family would call home for nine months. Amber didn't like the way the trees looked or the things she saw hanging from branches and scurrying off in the underbrush.

She held tight to her brother's hand, wishing they didn't have the parents they did. Normal parents didn't make their kids tote Bibles in their backpacks or sleep on folding cots inches above a ground teeming with creepy crawlies.

Her skin itched from mosquito bites, but she didn't let Kyle's hand go.

"It'll be all right, Amber," he'd assured her. "I'm here for you. It'll be all right, you'll see."

And she had believed him. Always.

Except, it wasn't. Not then. And definitely not now.

Sniffling and banishing from her mind thoughts of that last painful missionary assignment, Amber followed the pickup truck in front of her. Her first impression of Community Christian Church's camp was that it was pristine—tranquil even. It looked more like a state park than the missionary sites she'd grown up in. Five large buildings—the middle and biggest one of them including a front porch and probably a lodge—were to the right. Picnic tables positioned under large pines were scattered about the area. A small pond, not really big enough for anything but a view, was to the immediate left. And off to the far left, she saw several paths leading to a copse of trees.

The pickup pulled in front of the large building where Nancy Baines waited. She waved and came to greet Amber.

"I'm so glad you were able to do this."

Wish I could say the same, she thought. "Not a problem," Amber said out loud. "I brought some gear with me, just in case."

"Oh, good. Just let me know if you need anything. Mess hall's over there," Nancy said, pointing toward the other buildings. "The last one."

"Thanks," Amber said. "I'll go take a look around."

"Manuel will help you get everything set up. He's our groundskeeper. He's around here somewhere."

"Right-o," Amber said.

No stranger to hard work, Amber figured she'd be on her own setting up the kitchen. Now all she had to do was find it.

"I don't want to sleep in the woods by myself," Sutton told Paul.

"You won't be by yourself, pumpkin. There'll be lots of people from the church and from your Sunday school class."

"What if they don't have a night-light like we have here at home?"

"I've packed one in your bag, with extra batteries. You can keep it next to your pillow."

Sutton didn't look at all appeased by the concessions.

Truth be known, neither was Paul. This camping trip was the first time he'd be away from the children since that angry, ugly night that brought them all together almost three years ago. The counselor he'd worked with in Los Angeles had said the first time would be tough. Paul just hadn't expected to feel as if he were abandoning them.

He poured milk for the kids and had started to put the carton away when he decided to have a glass for himself. He'd made meat loaf and mashed potatoes for dinner.

"How's that salad coming, champ?"

"Almost done," Jonathan reported. He plopped cherry tomatoes around the salad bowl, then admired his handiwork. "It looks too good to eat."

Paul chuckled. "Nice try, Jon, but you're eating it."

"I like salad," Sutton said from her perch on the counter.

"I know you do. Jon does, too. Right?"

The boy wrinkled his nose. "I hope they don't have lettuce at the camp."

Paul lifted Sutton up. "Don't forget the napkins."

"I already put them by each plate," the girl reported.

"Good job."

The small family sat at the table in the dining room of the house Paul bought in Wayside. Here, he'd been able to afford a real home with a backyard, the right sort of environment in which to raise his niece and nephew. In L.A., he'd been lucky to find a dump of an apartment to rent for the same price.

They held hands and Paul said grace. Over the meal, he again reviewed the rules about the camping trip.

The younger kids would be in a dorm, so he didn't worry about that. A list of what-ifs plagued him, though: What if Sutton had one of her nightmares? What if Jon started wetting the bed again? What if a snake bit? Or one of them got injured in a fall?

Get a grip, he told himself. He had done a site visit, had looked all around and deemed the camp a safe environment, just the sort of place he wished he'd had available while growing up.

"Let's run through the safety procedures one final time," he said. "What happens if somebody gets sick?"

"Find Mrs. Baines," the kids echoed.

"What if…"

"What if the boogeyman comes?" Jon said, a grin splitting his face.

Paul sucked in his breath, struck by how much Jon looked like his father had at that age, full of fun and mischief and big dreams for the future. But Mikey's future had been cut short.

"Daddy?" Sutton's voice was shaky.

"Don't tease your sister," Paul said, almost automatically. "And eat your salad, Jon."

"Why can't you come, too, Daddy?"

He'd been asking himself the same question. But Paul knew the answer. He couldn't baby them forever. This trip would be just as good for him as it was for them. While they made new friends and did arts and crafts, maybe Paul could practice using his own rusty social skills. The evening at Haley and Matt's house was the first time since moving to Wayside that he'd done anything with adults other than work. His heart wasn't in it, but maybe he'd call Marnie Shepherd and invite her to dinner or a movie or something.

"It's a camp for kids," he said, realizing how lame that sounded. "It's time for you to make some more friends."

"We'll make friends at school," Jon pointed out.

Paul had enrolled them in Wayside Preparatory, the private elementary school where Haley Brandon-Dumaine taught. School would start there the week after the camping trip.

"You won't hear Bible stories or sing around a bonfire at school. And remember," he said, "I'll be there family night. You can show me what you've learned."

"It'll be all right, Sutton," Jon said. "If something happens, I can call on the cell phone. Right?"

Paul tapped fists with the boy. "Right."

Sutton eyed the men. "Are you sure?"

Jon nodded, looking much older than his seven years. "Absolutely."

She didn't want to be here, but she'd given Haley and Kara her word. So Amber determined to make the best of a bad situation. She'd whip up some fabulous dishes and avoid all contact with the camp's program activities. She was here to do a job, not participate.

"Keep your mind on the job...and the money," she said.

One good thing that could be said about the mess hall at Camp Spirit Fire was that Community Christian Church didn't skimp on the cookware. She paused and took in the large kitchen with its large copper pots. Designed for a cook's easy movement and access to essentials, Amber couldn't fault it one bit. The mess hall's kitchen, fully equipped, met her picky standards. She ran a hand over the cool surface of a pan, and then the gleaming metal of an oven door. Everything she'd need was right here.

If she set up a cot over by door, she'd never even have to go outside. The mess hall at Camp Spirit Fire was set up for comfort in a pastoral setting. The outside of the building looked rustic, but the inside had serious amenities, right down to something that looked suspiciously like a satellite dish television connection in a little office off the kitchen. From what she'd seen so far—and that wasn't much since she hadn't taken any time at all to look around the place, and didn't plan to—it appeared to be a far cry from the backwoods campsites and cook fires she remembered from her youth—places with outdoor pits dug in the ground for stoves and no running water or indoor plumbing.

She found fault with just one thing here. Amber cast an unkind glance at industrial-sized cans of pork and beans. With *a lot* of doctoring she could make that edible—maybe.

"We're sure glad you were able to help out," said a voice behind a dolly filled with boxes. "Where would you like me to put these?"

"Are you Manuel?"

He poked his head around the load. "In the flesh."

"What is all that?"

"Fruit. Canned and fresh. I have a couple more loads. Oatmeal, breads. The milk, juice, eggs and stuff will come this afternoon."

Amber sighed. "Over there," she said, pointing toward a pantry. "Do you know when the mess hall volunteers arrive? I was told there'd be two people helping me."

"Sorry, don't know anything about that. Mrs. Baines has the volunteer list, though." He wheeled the dolly into the large pantry. "If you catch her, she'll probably be able to tell you. She's checking the tent sites."

"Tents?"

Hadn't Haley said something about dormitories? Amber had seen several buildings.

"Sure," Manuel said. "But only the senior kids are allowed to camp outside. Those who are going to graduate from high school in the spring do it as a tradition. You know, a last hurrah before college and jobs."

Amber nodded, relieved.

At first she'd planned to sleep in her own bed every night, then realized she hadn't given the logistics of this job much thought. To drive up here every morning to have breakfast ready, she'd have to leave home at three in the morning. It would be a long drive home at night, only to start the process over again before dawn.

Maybe she should have demanded quadruple rate.

Community Christian's annual youth camping trip was a tradition that the church's young people looked forward to each year. Held in early September, it was part revival and part final farewell to summer before buckling down seriously to a new academic year.

The church usually had about thirty children between the ages of five and eighteen participate in the weekend event that started with a Friday night jamboree and welcome. This year, however, Amber would be cooking for fifteen more kids, whom Kara Spencer's grant had enabled the church to include from various mentoring and outreach programs the church ran.

"Is Marcus going to be able to make it up this weekend?" Haley asked.

She and Kara were in the lodge in the back of the gathering room. Just as soon as a few stragglers got checked in, Cliff would open the weekend with prayer and a motivational message.

"Nope. He's really been putting in a lot of hours trying to get all of Patrice's tracks done for her CD. She's so excited."

"Being able to record like that has to be a dream come true for her."

Kara nodded. "It is. We're all so proud of her. My baby sister is going to be a gospel star. She's done all right for herself—"

"Excuse me."

They edged out of the way as Amber and Manuel pushed a large cooler in. "Popcorn and bug juice for the snack tonight," Amber said. "Real food in the morning."

Just as soon as they got the cooler situated, Amber wiped her hands on her jeans.

"Thanks again for agreeing to do this," Kara said. "I know you could have said no."

Amber grinned. Spending time in a kitchen always lifted her spirits. "What mortal could resist dual salvos from the dynamo twins?"

Haley and Kara shared a smile. Best friends for years,

the two women were not physically similar: Haley a tall, well-rounded blonde, and Kara a petite black woman with crimped hair and always-perfect makeup. Haley and Matt and Kara and Marcus looked like people who belonged on the covers of magazines. Heck, Marcus *was* on the cover of magazines! And as the R & B superstar's fiancée, Kara had been, too.

Next to Haley and Kara, Amber felt like a slouch. Though she and Haley had the same coloring and hair, her idea of a hairstyle was pulling her shoulder-length blond curls into a ponytail. She rarely, if ever, wore makeup. And while Haley always looked like she'd stepped straight out of a magazine ad, Amber had never met a pair of jeans that didn't speak to her. Even her work clothes for her catering business tended toward the practical—cleaned and pressed khakis with polo shirts that carried the Appetizers & More logo. If she had to dress up, she exchanged the pullover for a crisp white shirt with black slacks.

For the camping weekend, she'd opted for jeans, hiking boots, and chambray shirts and sweaters that could easily be worn in layers when the days and nights got cool.

At least this is easy money, Amber thought. And as long as she didn't let anything interfere with that, all would be well.

Nancy Baines, looking smartly efficient with clipboard in one hand and a pencil tucked over her ear, came up and hugged them all. Kara and Haley threw themselves into the embrace, while Amber leaned in awkwardly. She didn't like people touching her, but Nancy Baines reminded her a lot of her mom.

"Did you find Jocelyn's notebook?" Nancy asked. "She said she left it in the office so her replacement could find some of the recipes."

"I saw it," Amber said. "But I don't need it. I'm using my own recipes."

"Well, uh..." Kara started. "Remember, these are kids. They aren't expecting or looking for anything fancy."

With a wink and a smile Amber waved away the concern. "I have everything under control," she assured them. As a matter of fact, she'd already mapped out menus for the next two days.

Nancy patted her arm. "I'm sure you do. If you're missing anything, need anything, please," she said, "don't hesitate to ask." Then, turning to Haley and Kara, she asked, "Are you ladies staying overnight?"

"Can't," Haley said. "But we'll be back."

"I'm looking forward to my rap sessions with the kids this year," Kara said. "It's hard to believe some of them are graduating already."

Nancy nodded. "I see someone I need to speak with." She reached for Amber's hand and gently squeezed it. "Amber, I'm so glad you were able to help us out. You're truly a God-sent blessing."

Amber didn't like thinking of herself in those terms, so she quipped, "I was coerced," sending a grin toward Haley and Kara.

"Well, the Lord knew we needed you here," Nancy said. "Don't stay holed up in that kitchen all weekend. There's lots of free time. Join in on some of the activities."

"I love white-water rafting," Haley said. She placed a hand on her stomach. "But Matt won't let me do anything fun."

"I guess we won't be rock-climbing together this year," Kara said.

"Don't think so."

Nancy chuckled. "Don't let these two fool you with their tall tales," she said. "One of them—I won't name any names—decided last year that an outdoor excursion meant a sun chair and a novel over at the lake."

Kara laughed out loud. "I was exhausted from running after little kids that year."

Nancy nudged Amber and both women grinned. "See, she told on herself. I wasn't going to say which one—"

"Mrs. Baines?" A voice floated over.

"On the way," she called. "Seriously, though, Amber, please, join us for the campfire chats, any of the outdoor excursions, the Bible study. Whatever you feel led to do. Okay?"

Amber nodded. She was pretty sure, however, that she wouldn't feel "led to do" anything except the job she'd been hired to perform.

Twenty minutes later, lanterns lit the evening as Amber and all of the others stood or sat around the front pond. Cliff Baines welcomed everyone and then talked about finding yourself and helping others.

"Everyone attending this weekend gathering is here as a result of God moving in your life," the preacher said. "There are no coincidences." He leaned toward the younger children. "That means nothing happens by accident. Over the next few days, we're going to have some fun. We'll enjoy this beautiful camp area, eat some great food, enjoy the water and hiking trails, and then, when it's time to go home, we'll all leave refreshed and renewed. Ready to seriously hit the books," he added with a mischievous grin.

That last comment earned him plenty of groans.

"Let us enjoy the weekend without thinking about that," Adam said.

Chuckling, Cliff opened his Bible. "All right. It's a deal. Let me share this Scripture text with you. It'll be our focus for this weekend."

As he read a familiar passage from Proverbs, a chill shimmered through Amber. She tried to shut out his words—the words she knew so well.

A long time ago she used to trust in the Lord with all her heart. Until he let her down. Now, the only path she walked was the one she could see. Believing that God would see her out had almost killed her. Faith was not a concept she could count on or believe in.

"Hi, Cookie Lady."

She looked down to see Sutton Evans, and smiled. "Well, hi there to you, too. What are you doing here?"

"Camping!" The girl grinned. "You, too?"

"I'm the camp chef. I'll be cooking all your meals."

Sutton's eyes widened. "Cookies every day?"

Amber chuckled. "Maybe cookies on one day."

"Two days," the girl shyly bargained.

"We'll see."

When a group of teens with tambourines and a guitar stood up and started singing, a tiny hand found its way into Amber's. For a moment she was startled. She looked down at Sutton, whose eyes didn't miss a thing going on around her. But the little girl held on tight, as if she were afraid Amber might disappear.

If it weren't for Sutton, she just might. As she listened to the foot-tapping melodies that reminded her too much of similar nights in Central America, Amber tried to focus on the triple rate that would add to her bank balance, rather than the fact that once upon a time, Proverbs 3:5-6, the passage Cliff had just read to the campers, had been her favorite Scripture.

◆ Chapter Eight ◆

The youngest children, housed in King Solomon's Palace—each building had a biblical name—slept eight to a room on bunk beds. Sutton Evans didn't like the idea of being separated from Jonathan, who was across the hall. Jonathan's skills as a negotiator ultimately prevailed when he talked Mrs. Simmons, the dorm mom, into letting him sleep in the bunk closest to the door in the boy's room with Sutton in the corresponding spot in the girl's room. That way, just a little more space than what divided their bedrooms existed between them.

The hall light blazed, giving each child an extra measure of comfort.

"Do you have the phone?" Sutton double-checked—for the fifth time.

"It's right here," Jonathan assured her, patting his

robe. "When I get in bed, I'll put it under my pillow. It'll be okay, Sutton."

She bit her bottom lip, nodded. Later, as she padded to her own lower bunk, she still worried. Only five girls between five and eleven years old were at the camp, so they got to spread out a little in the room. And no one slept on the top bunk of Mrs. Simmons's bed.

Normally, all the boys were in two dorms and the girls in the other two. But the addition of the scholarship teens changed the makeup of the camp. With additional chaperones on duty and an adult in each room, Nancy and the camp board had decided to house the campers by age this year. If it didn't work out, they'd switch back next year.

While the other children settled in their beds, Sutton got on her knees to say her prayers. She could see Jonathan doing the same thing across the hall.

"Dear God, help me not be afraid to be in here by myself. And keep Daddy safe. Amen from Sutton."

Mrs. Simmons smiled. "That was a good prayer, Sutton. I'll tuck you in now."

Sutton looked at her but didn't say anything. She simply scampered into bed and pulled the cover up over herself and Wally, a stuffed plush fish with bug eyes and fuzzy rainbow fur.

"All comfy?"

Sutton nodded.

"Everybody settled?" Mrs. Simmons asked the room.

When she got affirmative answers from the girls, she said "Good night" and turned out the light.

Sutton flipped over on her stomach and looked toward Jonathan. He waved at her. Sure that everything was safe, considering that her daddy wasn't there, Sutton closed her eyes and fell asleep.

Amber did as much prep work as she could for the morning meal. She planned to serve waffles with peaches and a cream sauce for breakfast. She wasn't too happy that the peaches were canned and not fresh, but, given the season, she'd have to make do with a few substitutions. For lunch the next day, she'd decided on a bacon-and-cheese topped casserole that would at least get rid of some of the pork and beans in the pantry.

Her two assistants—high school students Kirsten and Leanne, both members of Community Christian— proved to be eager helpers. The girls were planning to study culinary arts after graduation, and by asking lots of questions they showed an interest in learning all they could from Amber over the weekend.

Confident that her meal plan included a variety of appetizing choices—with the exception of the pork-and-beans abomination—Amber finally made her way to the adult dorm, the one set aside for grown-ups who didn't have chaperoning duties.

As she walked across the compound, she could hear laughter and voices drifting on the quiet night. Though the hour was late, the teens and older kids who opted to sleep in tents or under the stars were apparently having a late-night gab session. She paused for a moment to listen to the snatches of conversation and laughter she heard, but couldn't quite make out what they were saying from this far away.

The sounds put her in mind of the natives whispering among themselves when the missionaries showed up with big smiles, open hearts and backpacks full of Bibles. Over time, she'd learned the languages and dialects, but in the beginning it had all been so foreign and frightening and seemingly pointless.

Growing up, Amber hadn't had many friends. Often, the local girls, wary of outsiders with a salvation agenda, ignored her attempts to make friends. In all her years, she'd been close to just two of the people at the missionary campsites. Ben who'd drowned while trying to save a puppy in a hurricane, and Angeline.

With a start, Amber realized she hadn't thought of her old friend in many, many years.

When her parents first got the Honduras assignment, they insisted that Amber and Kyle learn Spanish so that they could read and speak it fluently. The Spanish was the only good thing that lingered from those early years. It served her well, too well in fact, because speaking the language was how she'd met Raymond Alvarez.

Shaking off the melancholy brought on by lost years, forgotten friendships and continuing nightmares, Amber moved on.

The teens camping out apparently still had plenty of energy to burn. Amber couldn't say the same. All she wanted was a hot shower and then a bed that wasn't on the ground. On her shoulders she carried a sturdy backpack designed for rugged wear. One of the few things she'd kept from her missionary days, the pack had a bedroll attached, just in case. If nothing else, Amber knew how to prepare for the worst.

Checking her locker key and room assignment, Amber entered Joshua House. The thought of that hot shower propelling her, Amber found her room, one she'd share with three others. But four people were already sprawled across the beds. With duffel bags open and toiletry kits out, the four women looked as if they belonged there.

"Uh." Amber looked at her key and assignment again. "Hi."

"Hey, Amber," one of the women said in greeting. "What's going on?"

Amber glanced at them, all fresh-faced and energetic. She felt old, well beyond her twenty-nine years.

"I was trying to find my place— I mean my bed," she said. "This says Joshua House, Room 4, Bed 2."

"Oh, they didn't tell you?" One of the women scrambled up and reached for a tote bag. "I'm Jen, by the way."

Amber had a bad feeling about that breezy "didn't they tell you" comment. Though prepared for the contingency, the last thing she was of a mind to do was spend a cool Oregon night sleeping on the ground.

The others introduced themselves, including Betsy, a woman Amber remembered from earlier in the day. She'd let Amber know about a peanut allergy.

"There were some reassignments," she said. "We're the praise-and-worship team, so Mrs. Baines put us all together so we could practice a bit and go over what we need to do.

Jen came back with a sheet of paper. "This says you're in King Solomon's Palace. That's Building 5."

"Thanks," Amber said.

She trudged back outside, but stopped short on the front steps. She hadn't been paying too much attention while her chef assistants chattered in the kitchen, but she did recall that name. Wasn't King Solomon's Palace a kids' dorm?

Sleeping on the ground in the woods would be preferable to sharing sleeping space with children she didn't know how to relate to. The Cookie Lady persona she donned for an hour on Wednesdays was one thing; trying to maintain it for three straight days up here was another beast altogether.

When she got to the room Betsy and Jen had indicated, it was filled with four bunk beds.

"Hi, Amber. I wondered when you'd find your way over here."

Amber turned at the voice.

"I'm Harriet. We met earlier."

"Isn't this a kids' dorm?"

Harriet nodded, a smile on her face. "They're a good bunch. Most of them fell asleep about half an hour ago. Come on, I'll show you where we are."

She led Amber into the room filled with bunk beds,

unlike the accommodations for the adults. "Sorry there's no lower bunk available," Harriet said on a whisper. "I parked my stuff here, but I can move up if you'd prefer the bottom."

"It's not a problem," Amber said, but she was already counting the hours until she could get back to the security and comfort of her own apartment.

The only good thing was that she'd be up and out before the children really stirred. After a tepid shower, she climbed into the bed that was hers for the next few days.

Amber fell into a fitful sleep, dreams of Kyle and Guatemala, Honduras and hurricanes filtering through her. They ran through the underbrush, a headless man chasing them. She stumbled and fell, screamed when she landed on top of a snake.

The screaming continued. On and on.

Amber sat up, blinked and realized that the terrified sound, much like that of a trapped animal, hadn't been part of her dream at all. It was one of the girls.

She jumped down from her bunk.

"What? What?" Mrs. Simmons tossed her covers off, and several of the girls bolted upright and also started hollering, more from confusion than anything else.

But Amber was already there—at Sutton's side.

The child was having a nightmare, one that gripped her and wouldn't let go. She thrashed from side to side as if doing battle with something or someone.

"Daddy, don't let them shoot me. Don't let them take me."

"Sutton, wake up. Wake up."

Sutton's eyes opened, but she stared vacantly as if trying to figure out where she was and what had happened.

Amber lifted the girl into her lap, rocking her, soothing her any way she could think of. She knew what it was like to wake up in a strange place surrounded by strange people.

Barefoot and with his flashlight and cell phone in hand, Jonathan came running into the room. "What did you do to my sister?"

Sutton saw her brother and burst into tears, but she clung to Amber.

The phone rang and Paul snatched it up, rolling out of bed at the same time. "Hello? Jon? Sutton?"

"Sutton had a nightmare. A bad one. She says she wants to go home."

"I'll be right there."

Paul broke the speed limits he normally enforced, but got to Camp Spirit Fire in record time. The kids were supposed to be in the same bunkhouse, so he headed there first. But he couldn't find them.

Panic shot through him. He whirled around, ready to wake up everybody in the place.

"Chief Evans. Over here." A woman beckoned. "Hi, I'm Harriet Simmons, dorm mom and room 3 chaperone. Your kids are over in the kiva with Amber."

Paul blinked. With Amber?

He followed the woman to a common room. And

there, on a deep sofa, sat Amber with Sutton in her lap and Jonathan hovering nearby. Protecting the women.

Paul rushed forward. "Jon? Sutton? What happened?"

Amber cast wide eyes up at him, a tremulous smile on her face. "Just a bad dream— Right, honey?"

Sutton nodded.

"Your dad's here," she told the girl in a quiet tone.

Sutton didn't let go of Amber, but she held a hand out to Paul. "Amber made the monsters go away."

"Oh, baby. I'm sorry I wasn't here."

Sutton bit her lip. Paul held his arms out to her and the girl went into them.

He wrapped an arm around Jonathan, and hugged his two precious charges close. "I won't leave you alone again. I promise."

Caleb Jenkins drove by Marnie's house. The lights were on upstairs. He wondered what she might be doing and whether she would welcome her brother-in-law's company for a bit. His foot hovered over the brake pedal as he cruised the street.

An upstairs light blinked out. The two front rooms, he knew, were bedrooms.

Caleb didn't let his mind go there. Instead, he pressed the gas and hightailed it from the danger zone. That's what he'd come to think of Marnie as. As much as he loved her, he could never let her know. She'd been married to his brother—was still married to his brother as far as Caleb could figure. For a woman like her to remain shackled to a man like Roy could mean just one thing: she still loved him.

Roy didn't deserve any love. What he needed to be was dead. Just like all those kids he killed.

Conviction hit Caleb hard then. As a man of God, it wasn't his place to sit in judgment. But as a law enforcement officer, he knew his brother hadn't got nearly what he deserved.

"I'm sorry," he said, talking out loud to God. "It's how I feel. I can't make how I feel go away."

Yes, you can. The quiet conviction came from a place deep within.

He whipped his head around in the patrol car. No one was there, of course. No one at all. His windows were up. The AM/FM radio off. There hadn't been so much as a peep from his police radio in thirty minutes.

Caleb.

He heard the summons as clearly as if someone were in the vehicle with him. Caleb swallowed, and then sighed wearily. The old saying "You can run, but you can't hide" came to his mind.

Caleb pulled the squad car over. He left it running but cut the lights. Then he carefully placed both hands on the top of the steering wheel.

With his eyes closed and his head bowed, Caleb answered the summons. "Yes, Lord."

When he finished praying and meditating, he knew he'd be called to minister to a certain group of people— even though he didn't feel qualified.

* * *

Marnie stepped away from the window. The first time she'd seen the police car go down her quiet street, she hadn't thought anything of it. But the second time, and then the third time, she started to pay attention. Wayside wasn't all that big, and her street, a quiet established one, rarely saw traffic except for the people who lived there, let alone a police presence.

At first she'd thought someone had had a break-in. But the block's neighborhood watch system would have kicked in under that circumstance and she'd have gotten at least a phone call.

Then, this latest police car had paused. Right in front of her house. And she'd seen him. Caleb.

Marnie smiled. It was nice of him to check up on her like that. But Caleb needn't worry. Marnie knew how to take care of herself.

She turned out the light in the spare bedroom where she'd pulled out an overnight bag, then went to her own room.

Marnie had some decisions to make about her life. She loved her work at Sunshine and Rainbows, but had come to realize that she couldn't do that forever. She'd started working with kids as a way to give back what Roy took. But it was time to live her own life the way God meant for her to do. Marnie's faith was strong, but quiet—a hard-earned faith, tried and tested, that at times was all she'd had to cling to.

In the overnight bag she tucked the few things she'd

need for her two days and nights volunteering at Camp Spirit Fire. She planned to enjoy the weekend, since it could very well be her last at Community Christian's church camp. A new church family and experience awaited her. All she had to do was say yes to the opportunity she'd been given.

From her nightstand, she picked up the newspaper from Coos Bay, a town near the coast, about two hundred miles away.

This weekend she'd give some thought to the job offer. She'd give some *serious* thought to it. Her divorce from Roy was final, the decree on the way in the mail from her attorney in Portland. She'd even started using her maiden name again. All that tied her to Roy was the house they'd shared. She could sell it—had planned to do so anyway—and begin her life anew.

Coos Bay, Oregon, would be a nice place to start over.

Chapter Nine

Amber zapped water in the microwave and made cocoa for the children. Then, as unobtrusively as possible, she tried to slip away. It was going on one in the morning and she'd barely get four hours of sleep before it would be time to get up to start breakfast for the campers, counselors and chaperones.

"Miss Montgomery— Amber, would you wait?" Paul asked. "I want to have a word with you."

Her reluctance must have been evident, because he added "please" to the request.

"Let me get them back to bed, and I'll be right back," he said.

She nodded. While Paul saw to his children, Amber reached for a packet of cocoa, then filled another cup with water and put it in the microwave.

It took him longer than a minute. She'd moved outside, the temptation of that comfy sofa a lure she needed to resist if she were to stay awake while waiting for him.

The door opened behind her, and she turned. The police chief's powerful physique took her breath away. But for the first time, it wasn't in fear. Amber wondered what it might be like to be truly loved by a man like Paul. Paul Evans doted on his kids. He'd probably been the same way with their mother, Amber figured. The way Cliff and Nancy acted with each other. They'd been married for forever, but still acted as if they were dating.

He joined her at the railing where she'd been staring out at nothing while thinking complex thoughts that left her mind reeling. The portion of Cliff Baines's message that she'd heard tonight ran through her head, tormenting her with its upbeat sincerity and hope. Then there was Sutton. Why had the girl latched on to her the way she had?

"Thanks for what you did with the kids," Paul said. "I know it can't be every day that you have a hysterical five-year-old on your hands."

"She wasn't hysterical. Just a little scared after a bad dream."

"She has nightmares sometimes," Paul explained. "I had hoped they'd stopped. I think the excitement of the day and the new surroundings probably prompted this one."

"I know how that can be." Amber stared at the night sky for a bit, her mind still on the fireside message she'd heard earlier. "In his opening remarks, Reverend Baines said everything happens for a reason. Do you believe there's a divine order to the universe? That everything *really* happens for a reason?"

He nodded. "I do. Think what might have happened here tonight if we hadn't met at that crazy dinner-dance."

"Nothing would be different."

"Not true," Paul said, hitching a boot along one of the rails. "If we hadn't met that night, you'd be a stranger to me. I'd have been kind of freaked out to find my niece clutching some strange woman. But I knew you from that night. And Sutton and Jonathan, well, they know and trust the Cookie Lady. Before I even met her, I liked the Cookie Lady because she made my kids smile."

"That was before you thought she was holding a knife on you." Amber didn't dare touch the *I liked the Cookie Lady* part. Surely he meant it in a generic sort of way. So she ventured to other, safer territory that didn't involve her own life.

"Sutton's your niece? I didn't know that. What happened to them in L.A.? Jonathan started to explain, then said he'd better not."

Paul expelled a long breath.

"If you'd rather not get into it..." Though he looked pained, inside Amber was just dying to know what was up with those two kids.

"No, that's not it," he said. "It's such a long story."

"So give me the microwave version. Less time, less fat."

He smiled and leaned back, his hands behind him. "I was a cop in L.A. for many years, quickly moving up the ranks. I made a lot of collars—" he glanced at her "—that's arrests—of some pretty bad people."

Knowing the lingo, she nodded.

"The brother of one of them had been gunning for me for taking his gang leadership down," Paul said. "He took it personally and laid an ambush for me. But instead of taking me out, the hit he ordered killed my brother and his wife."

Aghast at what he related in such clinical terms, Amber stared at him. The anguish on his face told her, though, that the hurt still ran deep in him. She reached for his hand.

"I'm sorry. I know that sounds lame, but I don't know what else to say."

He sighed again.

"What happened?" Amber's question seemed loud in the quiet night, embers from the dying bonfire providing light and the occasional snap of wood.

"Mike and Sarah were staying at my place while their house was getting painted. Sarah was pregnant and they didn't want her exposed to the fumes. Somebody kicked the door a couple of times. They thought it was me with an armful of groceries.

"Mikey opened the door and got two bullets straight in the heart. Sarah came running and they took her out, too."

Amber gripped his arm. "Where were Sutton and Jonathan?"

"In the next room. They hid when they heard the shots. Jonathan is the one who called 9-1-1. He was holding Sutton and clutching the phone." Paul closed his eyes, his voice hollow, weary. "That's how the first units at the house found him. Sutton crying and screaming and trying to get to her mom, and Jonathan clutching the phone and Sutton."

She reached for his hand. "Oh, God. Those poor babies."

She closed her eyes, trying to imagine the horror of that day, sure that her worst imagining paled compared to what actually happened. Two innocent children witnessing the brutal slaying of their parents. How did they ever recover from that? Could they ever recover?

At least she now knew why Jonathan was so protective of Sutton. She hoped he'd always be there for his sister, unlike her own brother. Without even realizing she did it, she said a little prayer of comfort for the children.

"I was their only family," Paul said. "And it was my fault. Sometimes I don't know how we got through that first year. Jon had horrible nightmares. The sound of a car backfiring would make him grab Sutton and duck. And I was blaming myself. If their parents hadn't been staying at my house, they'd be alive today."

"You don't blame yourself anymore?"

"Oh, yeah. I do. But I've learned how to handle it a little better than I did that first year."

"Whatever happened to the guy?"

Paul gave a smile, but it wasn't a pleasant one. Amber

realized again just how intimidating he could be. The look on his face right now told her that vengeance—and maybe even revenge—had been exacted.

"He's right where he belongs," Paul answered. "On death row."

Later, back in bed, Amber thought about what Paul had told her. They had more in common than she'd initially believed. They had L.A. in common. The City of Angels hadn't been kind to either of them and they'd both sought solace in Wayside, a world away from everything that was California.

Amber woke up tired and cranky, but working on the meals for the day lifted her spirits considerably. She took special care whipping a vanilla cream sauce, and she taught her two eager assistants a few tricks to shorten preparation time in the kitchen.

Proud of their hard work, Amber wasn't prepared for the hit when the first group of hungry campers came in for breakfast.

"Ew! What's this white stuff on my waffle?"

She heard it so many times that she knew she was in trouble. She, Kirsten and Leanne had already made all but the last batch of waffles with peaches and the cream sauce.

The adults raved, but the kids and teenagers were having serious qualms. One in particular, a Daphne with unruly red hair and freckles, led the revolt. "Where's the scrambled eggs and sausage?" she demanded.

Many of the others quickly took up the chant, holler-ing for real food, for scrambled eggs and sausage.

Mrs. Baines hustled to the kitchen where Amber stood in the middle of the floor trying to regroup. "Amber, there's mutiny in the dining hall."

Amber paced. "I know. I know."

"We've been telling them that lunch will be more to their liking. Didn't Jocelyn leave the menu book for you?" Nancy hurried to the office, where she found the big three-ring binder and brought it out and put it on the prep table.

"Yes, I saw it," Amber said. "I told Haley and Kara this wasn't going to work," she muttered.

A chant swelled up from the dining hall. "We want sausage! We want sausage!"

"I'm not a short-order cook."

"Oh, dear," Nancy said. "I think I'd better page Cliff. Do you think lunch can be more…normal? I thought the waffles were great, but I'm not a kid. And this weekend is really about the children."

Amber nodded. When Nancy dashed back to calm the mutinous little scamps, Amber plopped onto a chair. "Maybe I should go home right now."

"You can't do that," Kirsten said. "What'll every-body eat?"

"Apparently, not my cooking."

Leanne, the other would-be chef, joined them. "This is my fifth year coming up here. We always kinda eat the same stuff. It's tradition."

Beaten in spirit, Amber sighed. "Hand me that binder."

She spent the next hour trying to convince herself that beans and franks, gruel and s'mores were good eating. At least none of her regular Appetizers & More clients were here to witness her humiliation.

By lunchtime, she'd just resigned herself to the task at hand, never mind her bruised ego or the meals she knew to be both delicious and nutritious. Forget the vegetable omelettes with applesauce-and-almond muffins, or the mixed grill with chicken and chutney. No honey pecan rolls for this undeserving crew. On a white board in front of the mess hall she wrote out the menus for the rest of the day.

Lunch: corn dogs, pork and beans, and French fries, pudding, and milk

Dinner: corn chowder and chicken strips, applesauce, and milk

Late-night snack: marshmallows, popcorn, juice

For her own lunch, Amber made a small fruit and chicken salad, garnished it with a few peaches and brewed a pot of coffee.

"So what do I have to do to get a plate like that?"

She looked up.

Paul Evans stood in front of her.

"I thought you went home."

"I did, but I came back up for lunch only to find I'd missed the kids' mealtime. Sutton's in an art class and Jon is getting a canoeing safety lecture. So I figured I'd try to find you."

She cocked her head. "Why?"

He held out a little blue gift bag. Blue and white polka-dot tissue paper peeked over the top. "I wanted to say thank-you formally for last night."

"You didn't have to buy me anything."

"I know. I wanted to." He offered the bag again. "I saw this in the window at one of the stores on Main Street and thought of you."

Amber tugged out the tissue paper and found inside a ceramic "cooking" angel with wire wings. The small piece of folk art featured a mini rolling pin in the angel's arm. Amber smiled. She'd seen and admired the piece at World Emporium, a specialty shop on Main Street.

"Thank you." She was so touched she didn't know what else to say.

"The sign out there says beans and fries for lunch," he said, indicating the entryway to the dining room. "But that looks really good. Not like any camp food I've ever had."

"That, apparently, was the problem," she muttered. Hours later she still smarted at the reaction to her breakfast.

"What was that?"

"Nothing." She glanced at her meal. "I can share."

He smiled. "I'm not going to take the food from your mouth."

"You're not. Have a seat. I'll make you a plate. Would you like some coffee?"

"Sounds great."

She didn't know why she suddenly felt so charitable toward him. Maybe it had something to do with the vulnerability she'd seen in him last night. Or maybe it was because he'd done something nice for her, knowing instinctively that the cooking angel in the store window might be something she'd like.

A few minutes later, Amber returned from the kitchen with chicken salad and peaches for Paul and a carafe of coffee. She picked up her fork, but paused when he started saying grace. Amber felt chastised at her lapse, but bowed her head.

"Thank you, Father, for bringing Amber into our lives. She's been a blessing, and I pray you'll continue to bless her heart and her hands. Amen."

Amber stared at him.

Paul smiled at her and picked up his fork. "I heard there was a revolt here earlier. I hope Sutton and Jonathan weren't a part of it."

She shook her head. "No. I think it was just a couple of people, but they were loud and vocal. The others just rode the tide to have me tarred, feathered and run out of camp."

"They're just kids," he said. "I'm sure they didn't mean any real harm."

Amber disagreed, but didn't say anything. She concentrated on the chunks of chicken in her salad.

"Will you answer a question for me?"

She glanced at him. "Maybe."

"How'd you get Sutton to talk to you?"

Amber blinked. She wasn't expecting that. She shrugged. "I don't know. I didn't do anything special."

"Yes," he said, reaching for her hand. "You did."

A little uncomfortable with his praise and his touch, Amber pulled her hand away and tried to change the subject.

He didn't let go, though. "Sutton doesn't talk very much, and rarely to people she doesn't know well. Yet, last night she was all over you."

"She just knows me from the day care center."

"Hmm" was all Paul said as he lifted his fork.

"Are you staying up here the whole weekend?"

Caught in the middle of a bite, he chewed and swallowed first. "This is really good," he said, indicating the salad. "I have a patrol shift, but I'll be back tonight and then I'll stay the rest of the time."

"Since when does someone at chief rank work patrol shifts?"

"You sound like you're familiar with the police hierarchy."

"Unfortunately," she mumbled under her breath as she bit into a slice of peach.

He looked curious.

She shook her head. "Nothing. Listen, I hate to eat and run on you, Chief. But I promised Marnie I'd go hiking with her today. I don't have a lot of free time here and I'd hate to waste the little I do have."

He nodded, conceding that she viewed being with him as a waste of time.

"I didn't mean to delay you. Don't worry about me," he said. "I'll clean up after myself."

She picked up the gift bag with the kitchen angel. "Thanks again. See ya." Amber rose, took her plate and mug and disappeared.

He waited, but she didn't come back through the dining area. Paul figured she'd slipped out a back door, much like she'd slipped out of the conversation when it turned to policing.

This time he would run a check on her. If for no other reason, he needed, as Wayside's police chief, to ensure that the elusive Amber Montgomery wasn't up here hiding from the law, and possibly putting the church's young charges—including his own children—at risk.

"I'm ready to talk now," Amber said. "But I don't want to hear any of that Jesus stuff. I'm not into that."

"Why?" Marnie asked.

The two women stood on a high bluff overlooking the valley. They'd hiked up one of the faint trails, chatting along the way and now stood at a lookout point. Though they were safe where they were, jagged cliffs and outcroppings reminded them of the danger below. Small brush and the beginnings of what might later be large Douglas firs grew out of the side of the hill.

"Because I got an earful of it growing up. Because Jesus wasn't there for me when I needed him."

"I meant, why do you want to talk now?"

"Oh." Expecting the evening to grow cool, Amber

had thrown a sweater about her shoulders. Now she twisted the ends of the sweater arms, tying and untying them. "I just meant... Look, this isn't easy for me."

Marnie sat on two logs lashed together to form a bench at the lookout point. "Do you know what the hardest part was for me?"

Amber didn't answer.

Not dissuaded by her silence Marnie continued. "For me it was feeling like I'd somehow failed the test of being a human being. That I couldn't even handle the basics of being a woman."

Amber stared out at the view. The only sounds between the two women were the late-afternoon creatures coming alive in the brush, chirping, croaking and hooting. "So, like, what happened to you?"

Marnie rubbed her hands on her jeans. "I was married to Caleb's brother, Roy."

Amber turned at that revelation.

"He had a drinking problem." After a moment, Marnie shook her head, editing that description. "No, he was an alcoholic and a mean one to boot." She smiled sadly. "When he wasn't drunk he was a terrific guy. But after the third or fourth or tenth beer he turned into a different man, one who was vicious and cruel, who cared only about his own needs. The world was supposed to revolve around Roy."

"You said you have scars. You mean emotional ones?"

Marnie nodded. "Those, too." She shrugged out of her jacket, then lifted her sweater and T-shirt to reveal several small round scars on her stomach and side. Amber stepped closer to peer at them.

She reached a hand out, but didn't touch Marnie's skin. "What is that?" she asked gently.

Pulling her clothes down, Marnie said, "When he got drunk, I was Roy's human ashtray. I have some on my arm as well."

Horrified, Amber just stood there. No words formed in her brain as she struggled to process what she'd just seen and heard.

"Why'd you stay?" She asked Marnie the same question she'd asked herself over and over.

"I didn't have anywhere else to go. I thought it was my fault that he was the way he was."

Amber considered that. "Why didn't you tell Caleb? He seems like a decent enough sort."

"Tell him what?" Marnie countered. "That his adored big brother used me as a punching bag? That I was a failure as a wife? That I couldn't manage my own household and affairs? A part of me believed it was my fault. That if only I were a better housekeeper, a better cook, a better lover, maybe my husband would love me enough to stop hurting me."

"So, do you still think those things?"

"No," Marnie said. "But I did for a long, long time."

Amber stared at Marnie, then carefully asked, "What made you see things differently?"

"Three things. A good counselor, someone who specialized in domestic violence issues. A shelter where I met other women like me. And the love of a man who gave His all for me."

"Caleb?" Amber asked.

Marnie shook her head. "No, Amber, it was Jesus who gave His all for me."

A day ago, even a week ago, Amber might have bristled at Marnie's answers. But today she soaked them in, thinking about what she'd said. Kara had given her the name of a counselor who could be trusted. Amber still had the little piece of paper on which the telephone number had been written.

She'd never used the services of an emergency shelter, though now, looking back, she realized she should have. She had even known of one near where she lived in L.A. A neighbor had slipped her their brochure one day in the laundry room.

Amber blinked rapidly and her heart swelled. She'd been sent a message that long-ago day. The woman had tried, in the only way she knew how, to help. But Amber hadn't recognized the Lord's hand in the woman's gesture. Instead she'd just angrily tossed the brochure in the trash, had told the woman to mind her own business and had gone back upstairs—where Raymond beat her that night for forgetting to bring the stain remover upstairs from the laundry room. Though she'd run downstairs to get it, he claimed a stain had already set in his uniform and that it was all Amber's fault.

"I'm sorry," she said.

"There's no need to be sorry," Marnie said.

Surprised for a moment to even see Marnie there, Amber just looked at her friend. Her thoughts had been back in L.A., in that apartment complex—the apology meant for the neighbor who'd only tried to help.

Amber faced the lookout point again. "What happened to him? Your husband?"

"An accident. His fault, of course," Marnie said. "He was drunk and hit a van filled with children from Corvallis coming home from a band competition."

Amber faced her again, standing in front of a boulder next to Marnie. If she'd had any softness in her she'd have put her arm around the other woman's shoulders. But Amber didn't know how to do that.

"They died, didn't they?"

Marnie nodded. She blinked several times and tried to wipe the side of her eyes without Amber seeing the moisture there. "Everybody but Roy. I've lived my life since that day in service to children. In a way, doing penance for Roy's mistakes."

Amber turned her back on Marnie. "If Jesus was your Savior, where was He when your husband was putting his cigarettes out on your stomach?"

Marnie didn't take offense at the belligerent tone. She simply smiled. "I'm here today, Amber. That's testimony to the fact that His love kept me, even through the worst of it. Many, many nights I thought about just killing myself. Swallowing a whole bottle or two of the painkillers I hoarded for the burns."

Amber shook her head, not getting it. "Why didn't

you just…you know, end it all?" She'd sure considered that on more than one occasion while she lived with Raymond.

"Because I had so much more to live for. So much more to do."

Amber thought about that. Was the Lord's hand even in that? *Could Marnie have been spared just so she could be on this Oregon mountain today to talk to me?* The very notion seemed incredible. Yet Amber couldn't deny the possibility.

"You're still married?"

Marnie shook her head. "Not now. But it didn't seem right to divorce him right after the accident. I was his wife. He needed help. But I eventually needed some closure, some way to reclaim my own sanity."

"How can you stand it?"

"Which part?"

"All of it."

"I'm at peace with my past, Amber. I've forgiven Roy for what he did to me, what he stole from me."

"But how?"

"I found a Savior," Marnie said. "He was my lawyer, my comforter and my provider."

"Caleb?"

Marnie shook her head. "Jesus, Amber. Jesus saved me from the misery of my life."

Amber stood up again and walked to the very edge of the lookout. "I'm not into the Jesus thing." But this time, the words didn't carry quite as much conviction as before.

Marnie stood. "Amber, please be careful over there. Rock slides aren't unheard of around here. If you lose your footing, it's a long way down."

Amber stared out at the valley and the rushing river way below. "Yeah, I know." She glanced over her shoulder at Marnie. "But there is a way back up."

The corners of Marnie's mouth tilted, and Amber knew Marnie realized she hadn't been referring to the mountain.

Caleb Jenkins wrestled with the call that had been put on his spirit the night before. He'd sat in his patrol car for a long time struggling with the mandate he'd been given. His heart still had a hard time embracing the idea, but Caleb had run from God before, only to discover that everywhere he went, God was there, too.

The calling placed on him now seemed counter to everything he knew, everything he wanted in his life. But he didn't doubt, not for even a single moment, that his summons had been a divine one.

He drove out to the minimum-security facility where his brother Roy would be housed for the next twenty years.

In the beginning, while awaiting trial, Caleb visited his brother on a regular basis. Then he found out what Roy had done to Marnie. He'd found out by accident. She'd been having a heated discussion with Roy's lawyer in the courthouse. Caleb, waiting for the jury to return, overheard just enough to make him angry.

But when Caleb confronted Roy in his jail cell, Roy denied everything that Marnie had said. Marnie offered Caleb no explanation, simply saying that some things were between a husband and wife.

He'd never got up the nerve to ask her again about what he'd overheard her say to the lawyer. Caleb had his suspicions, though. And he knew enough to want to kill his brother for hurting Marnie. Even now, though what he felt toward Roy didn't qualify as homicidal, his feelings did make the new calling on his life all the more difficult to embrace.

Caleb believed the Lord wanted him to minister to the incarcerated. He knew he'd need to return to school for chaplaincy training, but doubted there'd be a class to deal with his particular issue. Prison chaplains weren't supposed to harbor ill will against the incarcerated. He just didn't think he'd be able to get beyond what his own brother had done.

If he followed through on the path he'd been called to walk, this could be his last opportunity to talk to his brother, to find out what happened, and maybe to reconcile with the brother he cherished as a child—the one who'd killed four kids and two adults but didn't walk away from the accident that took their lives.

Before long, he was sitting across from Roy. "How are you?"

Roy scowled. "How the hell do you think I am?"

Caleb prayed for some patience. He knew it wasn't easy for Roy. Being a convict had its own stresses, and

Roy had added ones on top of the normal prison pressure. But he was housed in a facility that could see to his needs.

"I just wanted to come check on you."

Roy eyed his brother, then said something profane. "What'd you really come up here for? Did Marnie send you?"

Caleb shook his head. "I'd like an explanation. You owe me at least that, Roy. Just tell me why you hurt her. What'd she ever do to you?"

"I knew she sent you up here. I don't owe you squat, little brother. Why'd you even come?"

"I came because I need some answers," Caleb said.

"Well, I ain't your teacher, so go get your answers somewhere else."

Caleb looked at the man he'd worshiped for so long. For most of their lives they'd been as close as brothers could be. Then things changed. Roy started hanging out with a different crowd. Somewhere along the way he'd met and married Marnie. Things were going well—or at least it seemed that way from the outside. They'd moved home to Wayside, bought the big house on Maple, and everything seemed great. They'd even joined a church, though Roy frequently found reasons not to go to services.

The change was so gradual Caleb didn't notice at first. Then one day he looked up and the vibrant, pretty Marnie he'd danced with on her wedding day was a woman who shrank into shadows and wouldn't accept hugs. On some level, he'd suspected then, but couldn't make himself believe that Roy, his idolized brother, was thumping on Marnie.

He'd asked her once, and she'd laughed it off, the old sparkle again in her eyes. He'd let it go then, because he didn't want to believe it could be true. Then came the accident. Then the trial. Then the words spoken in privilege to Roy's lawyer. His brother came crashing down from the pedestal upon which Caleb had placed him, shattered pieces all that remained.

Roy had killed innocent people and he'd tried to kill the spirit of the woman Caleb loved.

Caleb despised Roy for everything he'd done, everything he'd allowed himself to become. But Caleb couldn't deny blood. So he did his family duty by visiting Roy. Caleb, however, couldn't help wondering how they'd come to this pass—brothers who were strangers with nothing between them except harsh words.

"I miss the old Roy," Caleb said.

"Yeah? Well so do I."

"Why'd you do it, Roy? Why'd you hurt Marnie?"

Roy stared him down, his eyes cold and unfeeling. Just like his heart.

"Go to hell, Caleb." He twisted around and yelled for the prison attendant, who pulled his wheelchair away from the visitation table.

Caleb watched as the man who used to be his brother was wheeled away. Maybe he'd never truly understand what motivated Roy. All Caleb could do was pray for him, pray that one day Roy would face what he'd done and repent his sins.

Roy, Caleb knew, didn't think he was particularly lucky. But he was. He was still alive. Six people lost their lives in the drunken driving accident he'd caused. Roy Jenkins had survived, but without his arms or legs.

❧ Chapter Ten ❧

Marnie and Amber arrived back at base camp in time to see two girls pushing and shoving each other.

"Uh-oh," Marnie said.

"That doesn't look like fun and games to me," Amber said as they approached the lodge.

Then one of the girls threw a punch that knocked the other to the ground.

Amber and Marnie started running, as did two other counselors coming from the opposite direction, one on a walkie-talkie. Some of the children, the younger-age group that had been headed to the pond for fishing lessons, crowded around to see.

"Hey, break it up."

Adam Richardson grabbed the puncher, while Amber and Marnie helped the downed girl up.

"What's going on here?" Adam asked.

"She started it!"

"Did not!" Daphne hollered back.

"Did, too!"

The girls scrambled for each other, but were held back.

"Knock it off, guys," Adam said. He motioned for some help from Cindy, who'd herded the little ones together.

"She's just trying to ruin it for all of us!" Tanita, one of the girls, hollered.

"All right. That's enough," Cliff said, approaching with Nancy. "What happened here?"

"I was just minding my own business—"

"Were not. You said my tennis shoes had holes in them."

"They do."

The girls tried to scuffle again, but Adam held tight, as did Amber and Marnie. It took several minutes to sort out just what had happened between the girls, mostly a string of juvenile insults.

"I'm disappointed in both of you," Cliff said. "You two, come with me."

Nancy directed her attention to the children with fishing poles who'd witnessed the tussle. Some looked interested while others looked either shocked or frightened. One little girl was crying. Nancy went to her and knelt down, putting an arm around her while addressing all the others.

"What just happened here is not how we settle differences. Let's all go sit by the pond and talk about this."

"I want to go home," the girl said.

"All right," Nancy told her. "Let's go talk and then we'll see if you still want to leave. Okay?"

When the girl nodded, Nancy turned to lead the group of children, who'd started to mutter among themselves, to the lake.

The sound of sirens pierced the air and everyone turned to look. A moment later, two Wayside squad cars and an ambulance spit gravel and dirt as they flew up the road leading to the camp.

"Now look what you did!" one of the girls yelled, as she struggled to get to the other. "They're gonna send us to jail."

Cliff looked around. "Who called the police?"

The little crowd in front of the lodge stared open-mouthed at the five police officers and EMTs running toward them, Chief Evans leading the way.

He assessed the scene quickly. "What happened? Who's hurt?"

Seeing nothing truly amiss except two girls being restrained, Paul turned to Cliff, but scanned the group of children around Nancy. "What's wrong?"

Cliff motioned for another of the adult counselors to take the two girls to the camp office. Amber released the girl and stepped aside.

"Chief Evans, no one's injured," Cliff said. "There was a disagreement between a couple of the girls." The minister looked around and again asked, "Who called the police?"

"I did" came a quiet voice.

All eyes turned to the porch of the lodge.

Jonathan stepped out from behind a rocking chair, Sutton next to him. The two were holding hands, both children's eyes wide and frightened.

"They were fighting," Jonathan said. "I dialed 9-1-1."

Tears welled in Amber's eyes. "Oh, Jon."

She ran up to them and enveloped the two kids in her arms.

Paul felt the knot in his gut loosen. It had twisted his stomach the entire interminable time it took to get to the camp. That 9-1-1 call from Jon's cell phone had taken ten years off his life.

"You guys can head on back," he told the officers and paramedics. "May I have a word with you, Cliff?"

The minister nodded.

Amber brought Sutton and Jonathan to him. As they followed Cliff Baines, Amber heard Paul's words to his son.

"We need to have a talk about that phone, sport."

"Yes, sir."

After a conversation with Cliff in one of the rooms near the office, Paul brought Sutton and Jonathan in for a sit-down.

"You can't keep calling the emergency number, Jon."

"But it looked like they were going to hurt each other."

Paul struggled to find the right words. On the one hand, he wanted Jon to be proactive, to not allow himself to become a victim. On the other hand, there were limits that needed to be established.

"Nine-one-one is for emergencies," Paul said. "For when you need help. A car accident, a fire, a shooting." Both children shuddered at that example, but Paul forged ahead. "Help was here. Adam and Pastor Cliff and Mrs. Baines were handling the situation, weren't they?"

Jonathan nodded.

"What if there were a real emergency in town and the police were all up here? The people who really needed help might get it too late."

"I don't want that to happen," Jon said.

"Then, only use the emergency number when there's a true emergency, all right?"

Jonathan nodded. Sutton did, too.

Paul didn't want to do what he knew needed to be done next. He held out his hand. "I need the phone, Jon."

The boy's lips trembled. "But…"

"Campers here aren't even supposed to have them," he said. "I asked Pastor Cliff for a special exception for you after last night. But I can't justify that again, not when it's against the rules to begin with."

"I won't do it again."

"I know, sport. But I'm still going to hold on to it until the jamboree is over. Okay?"

With shaking hands, as if he were saying farewell to his best friend, Jonathan handed over the cell phone.

"What if there's an *emergency?*" Sutton said, accenting the last big word. She put her arm around her brother.

"I trust that Pastor Cliff and Mrs. Baines will be able to handle anything that comes up."

The kids gave him looks that said they weren't so sure about that.

Before dinner, Nancy called a meeting at the lodge of all the teen counselors, advising them of what Reverend Baines planned to do at the campfire chat that night and how to then answer questions that might come up in the dorms that evening. After the teens dispersed to go eat, she asked the adults and Adam to stay behind.

"The additional children this year have presented us with a unique problem," she said. "Something we didn't anticipate, but should have. We just opened our doors without considering that some of our scholarship children might have development needs. We did something we shouldn't have done."

"What was that?" a parent asked.

"We assumed they'd all know and adhere to the common courtesies we take for granted. If we do this again next year," Nancy said, "we'll look at possibly having a daylong pre-camp orientation instead of just the one-hour welcome tour."

"I think it was the right call to let both Daphne and Tanita stay," Adam said.

"Why is that?" someone asked. "Troublemakers are troublemakers."

Unsure for a moment, Adam glanced at Nancy. "Go

on," she encouraged him. "I asked you to stay because I wanted to get your perspective as the lead teen counselor."

"When we do outreach ministry in East Wayside," Adam said, "sometimes we come up against people who don't dislike us just because we're there to talk about church and Jesus. They don't care what we're saying— they don't like us simply because they don't know us. We're strangers speaking what, for some, is a completely foreign language. They've never been exposed to church. All they know is what they already know."

He paced the area in front of the large stone fireplace. "I talked to the girls," he said. "Tanita Jackson and her sister have never had an opportunity like this. They're both excited to be here. Those twins have never been to a camp like this. They've never been anywhere. What happened between them and the others, I think, grew out of fear."

"What's to fear?"

"Everything," Marnie said, from where she sat on the arm of a crate chair. "I remember the first time I went camping. I was with my parents, but the woods were scary. Add a bunch of strangers and forced activities." She shrugged. "It might be pretty scary to a thirteen-year-old, especially if she's already insecure about fitting in."

"And that's why Daphne Gregory picked a fight with Tanita," Adam said. "I think Miss Shepherd is right. It's a fear factor."

Nancy nodded. "Well, keep an eye out," she told them.

"Every year presents an issue. Let's hope that this one was ours for the weekend and that everything from here on out will be smooth sailing."

"Remember that time when the talent show team forgot that Jody was zipped up in that sleeping bag and he was jumping around like a cricket?"

The group started laughing at the recalled incident.

"Or when the skunk sprayed Pastor Cliff?"

Everyone groaned and then laughed at that.

"Pastor Cliff didn't think it was funny," Nancy said, but amusement laced her voice. "I made him sleep in the guest room for two nights until the stench completely faded." Nancy checked her clipboard to make sure she hadn't forgotten to tell them anything. "You guys go get some dinner. I'll join you shortly."

Still chuckling and talking about previous camping trips, the group dispersed.

Nancy went in search of Cliff and found him in the little office he claimed as a study while in residence at Camp Spirit Fire.

"Did we do the right thing?"

Cliff nodded. "I had a talk with both girls. I think everything will be all right between them now."

Nancy rubbed his shoulders and back, working the kinks out. "Then, why are you still so tense?"

"It's not them I'm worried about," he said. "It's Jonathan and Sutton Evans."

"What's wrong with them? Sutton is such a sweet little girl. She doesn't say much, but she has a gentle spirit."

"Too quiet and gentle for a five-year-old."

Nancy paused in her massage. "What are you saying?"

"I talked to Chief Evans," Cliff told her. "He's going to stay up here for the remainder of the weekend. This is the first time he's ever left them alone since the shooting." When Paul joined Community Christian Church, he told his new pastor about his own background as well as the children's. Cliff had kept the small family in his prayers ever since.

"Those poor babies. What they need is a mom. Someone to love them and give them hugs all the time."

Cliff glanced over his shoulder at Nancy. "Funny you say that. I was just thinking the same thing."

"Haley paired him with Marnie."

Cliff, a matchmaker in denial, shook his head. "I think it's Amber."

"Amber Montgomery?" Nancy's tone carried incredulity. "I don't see that. Amber is so...well, Amber."

"What's wrong with her? She's pretty. A great cook. And did you see the way those kids cling to her?"

Nancy had to concede that point. "She just doesn't seem like the hearth-and-home type, despite the baking."

"You're just comparing her to Haley, who is all of those things."

"True," Nancy said. "But you know she doesn't like men like Paul. He's a police officer, and the chief of police at that."

"Love has a way of overcoming those things," Cliff

said. "Since he'll be staying here, you'll get to see something I've seen."

"What do you mean?"

Cliff just smiled. "Check out the way they look at each other when they think no one's watching."

Amber had them ready, but no marshmallows would be roasted around the fire tonight. Snacks would be served in each of the kivas or at the tents. With Kirsten and Leanne, Amber made fast work of distributing bags of the sweet treat along with juice boxes to each of the sites. The teens then hurried to the campfire, where Pastor Cliff had just started his message. Amber followed.

"About eight years ago, my wife and I moved to Wayside. We'd been here before because we owned a little land not far from here, though we'd never spent a lot of vacation time in the area. We came up from Salem when the Lord called us to minister in Wayside."

With Bible in hand, he encompassed the entire group of children, teenagers and adults with his gesture. "We didn't have friends in Wayside because we didn't know anyone. But over time, we developed friendships, and we work at maintaining those relationships. It takes time and effort to have and keep your friends."

He looked out over the group. "You may wonder why I bring all of that up. It's because I wanted to illustrate to you that everyone, at some point, starts out as the newcomer—the person nobody knows."

Amber looked at her toes.

"Over time, Mrs. Baines and I met people, made friends and became a part of the community. And in this sense, I mean the Wayside community as well as the family of Community Christian Church. That's what we are, you see, a family. All of us here are a part of a large family."

He motioned for Nancy to join him. She did, and the two held hands. "Sometimes the two of us disagree."

"That's the truth," Nancy said to chuckles in the crowd.

"But that doesn't mean we ever stop loving each other."

"That, too, is true," she said.

Cliff kissed his wife's cheek. When she moved to sit, he continued to hold her hand.

"When Mrs. Baines and I have differences, we don't slug it out with each other. We sit down and talk about how we feel, how we can work out a solution to whatever the problem is. And we also pray together, as a couple and as individuals."

He released her hand then, and Nancy slipped back to her seat. "When we go to God in prayer, we turn to another family member, our Father. How many of you know 'The Lord's Prayer'?"

Hands shot up all around the camp. Cliff nodded. "Excellent," he said. "Excellent."

Opening his Bible, he turned to a passage in the New Testament. "The directions on how to say that prayer are in the Bible. You can find it at Matthew 6:9-13. Through His word, the Lord told us—in other words He taught us—how we should properly pray. Instruction isn't rebuke." He leaned toward the youngest children and asked, "Does anyone here know what *rebuke* means?"

A few heads nodded. "Max, stand up and tell us."

Max Young jumped up. "To rebuke means to fuss at."

Cliff nodded, and several of the adults smiled. "Yes, I suppose so. Good job, Max."

The boy beamed and sat back on the ground.

"We begin 'The Lord's Prayer' by saying 'Our Father...' Right?" More nods. "Well, if we say that, and mean what we're saying, we're acknowledging a Father in heaven who we report to. Just like you have to report to your moms, your dads, your grandparents or other adults in your household, as well as your teachers at school.

"As a family, we've been coming to Camp Spirit Fire for five years. When you're here, you are family no matter what other family you have back at the place you call home. Everyone here has equal access, to the facilities and the food. Equal access to all the activities because we provide for your needs while you're here."

He looked around, his gaze pausing on each of the young people who'd come to the camp as a result of the grant proposal Kara Spencer had written. "And each member of the family has equal access to both acceptance and forgiveness. But forgiveness doesn't just come out of the blue. You have to do something to get it. Does anyone know what that is?"

Several kids, including Max, raised their hands high. Cliff spotted Jonathan Evans among them and called on the quiet boy. "Tell us, Jon."

Jonathan stood up. "You have to say you're sorry and mean it," he said.

Cliff put an arm around the boy's shoulders. "Exactly. Jon is exactly right. So tonight, before lights-out in the dorms and at the tent camp, I hope you'll all have some conversations about family acceptance and forgiveness."

Amber stood listening to Cliff, marveling at the way he talked about what they had done to her and about the incident with the girls, but without making anyone feel singled out.

She watched as Jonathan tugged on the pastor's sleeve. When Cliff bent down, Jonathan told him something. Amber had a pretty good idea that it was probably an apology about the phone. When the two hugged, she smiled.

And she thought about her own family—not just Kyle whom she'd lost contact with and missed desperately, but the parents she refused to see or speak to. They had done what they thought was best.

Maybe it was time for her to ask their forgiveness.

❦ *Chapter Eleven* ❦

The last thing Amber wanted to do was open her heart again. The last time she'd done so, it had almost cost her her life. But she'd listened to Pastor Cliff, and pondered his words long after all of the others left. For the first time in many years, Amber began to consider that maybe God hadn't forsaken her back in L.A.

She felt Paul approach from behind. She didn't need to turn around to confirm it was him. Something in her spirit recognized him.

"May I join you?"

She waved a hand over the free bench. The campers, counselors and chaperones had all returned to their dorms or camp areas. But Amber still sat near the bonfire, enjoying the warmth cast by its dying embers.

"A penny for your thoughts."

"A penny doesn't get you anything these days," Amber said.

He dug in his pocket. "Well, how about a Camp Spirit Fire 'buck.' Sutton gave it to me and told me to buy myself a treat."

Amber smiled. "Keep your money, Chief. I understand you'll need that if you want extra goodies at the talent show Sunday. How are Sutton and Jonathan?"

"Wiped out." He settled on the far end of the bench where Amber sat, and rested his elbows on his thighs as he, too, stared at the burning wood. "I confiscated Jon's phone."

"The kids aren't supposed to have cells and pagers up here," Amber said. "The focus is supposed to be on God and nature. I heard them tell all the teens to keep them packed up. It probably never crossed anyone's mind to check with the little kids, too."

They remained quiet for a moment. Amber never shied away from asking the questions on her mind. In that regard, she might have made a halfway decent journalist. So she asked Paul the question that, to her, seemed obvious. "Why does a seven-year-old boy have a phone in the first place?"

Paul sighed. "I suppose it's my fault," he said. "Jon has some protection and safety issues that linger from the shooting. For him, having a phone at the ready means help is always available. I'd hoped this weekend would be the beginning of a little independence for them, especially Jon. Maybe I rushed things a bit."

Paul wasn't sure why he was telling her all of this. Despite her standoffishness where he was concerned, Amber seemed open and nonjudgmental when it came to children, his in particular.

She glanced his way. "It must have been hard for you."

"What?"

"Going from single guy to single dad with two kids."

He shrugged. "The Lord doesn't give us more than we can bear."

"Hmm." Amber stared at the fire, then glanced at him. "Something tells me you went through a lot before you could say that."

His steady gaze seemed to bore into her. He opened his mouth as if to say something, closed it, then just shook his head. No one else had ever sensed that in him. With a start, Paul realized that the pretty but skittish woman, who was so quiet about her own life, knew more about him than most people.

"You'd be right," he said, finally answering her.

They were quiet for a few moments.

She glanced at him. In jeans, hiking boots and a sweater, he didn't look nearly as intimidating as he did when he had on the blues and the holster that marked his profession.

"You changed. What happened to your cop gear?"

"Manuel ran me home to get some clothes and my truck."

"So you're staying up here?"

Paul nodded. "Manuel's going to put me to work. He said he can use another pair of hands."

He would be at the camp the rest of the weekend. Amber processed that information, and couldn't decide if that gave her comfort or made her nervous.

"Jon and Sutton will be glad to have you around."

"I'm going to try to give them some space. Instead of being just a cell call away, I'll be within hollering distance."

Amber smiled. "Did you really confiscate the phone?"

"It's in the back of my SUV."

She sighed, taking in the night. "He reminds me of my brother Kyle. We used to be close like that."

"Used to be?"

Amber shrugged. "We grew up and went our separate ways. The last time I saw him was..." She paused, trying to remember. Then, shaking her head, she said, "It's been about five or six years. The last I heard he was somewhere in Asia, following in my father's footsteps."

"Teaching?"

Amber laughed, but the sound carried a sardonic tone. "Preaching."

"You're a preacher's kid?"

She glanced over at him. "Don't go getting any ideas about PKs. I'm not that kind. My parents were missionaries."

"That must have been pretty cool."

She huffed. "Only if you like getting eaten alive by mosquitoes and other creatures or never knowing whether your bed will be the ground or a hammock high up in a tree. I didn't want to come up here for exactly that reason."

Paul peered up at the nearby trees, including some towering Douglas firs that had weathered many a Pacific Northwest storm. "I don't think they make anyone sleep in the trees here."

Amber chuckled, in true amusement. "No. But everything else is the same. Well," she added, "almost everything. The kitchen and mess hall are pretty spectacular. I'm a last-minute replacement and was expecting to have to cook over an open fire or a pit in the ground."

"I admire you," he said.

She turned questioning eyes toward him. "For what?"

"For agreeing to come up here not even knowing what the conditions would be like. If you were ready to cook meals for all these people over a campfire, you must be pretty resourceful."

Amber was quiet for a moment, bemused by the compliment. She'd never thought of herself as resourceful. She simply lived her life day by day, just trying to survive, trying to maintain some semblance of control over what happened to her.

But things weren't always in her control. She'd learned that lesson the hard way.

"Did you hear the campfire message Reverend Baines gave tonight?"

"Not all of it," Paul said.

Amber glanced at him, then reached for a twig and twirled the edge of it in the dirt at her feet. "Do you believe that stuff?"

"Which part?"

"About family and acceptance?"

"I have to," Paul said. "Otherwise, everything that I do, everything that I am is invalid."

She studied his profile in an attempt to figure out where he was coming from.

Amber, neither naive nor inexperienced, knew when a man was interested in her. Until now, none of the interest sent her way by the single men in Wayside had been reciprocated on her part. This cop's reluctant but apparent attraction both baffled and frightened her—even while it intrigued her.

Too many thoughts crowded her head: Paul, who was not only a cop but also the town's top cop. Her parents who'd treated her like a pariah. The brother who'd abandoned her, gone off seeking his own destiny. And Paul's children, Sutton and Jonathan, clinging to her today.

Too many emotions, too much to sort through. Amber didn't like complications. *Keep it light,* that's how she preferred it. Too many quandaries lurked below the surface.

Between Pastor Cliff's message that sent her out here to think and Paul's questions that rustled up the past, Amber figured she'd done way more than enough deep diving for one weekend.

"Reverend Baines decided not to expel the girls who were fighting," Paul said, breaking into her thoughts. "But they aren't in the same bunkhouse anymore."

"That's probably smart."

Amber stood up. "Listen, a friend of mine will be up here tomorrow. Well, actually, she's my cousin Haley's best friend. But, anyway, you might want to let her talk to Jonathan and Sutton."

"Why would I do that?"

"She's a shrink. No, they're the ones with the medical degrees, right? Kara is a Ph.D." Amber shrugged. "But even if she wasn't, she's good to talk to."

He caught her hand before she disappeared. "So are you."

Amber's breath hitched, and she immediately tried to pull away, but his words halted her. "I..."

"Thank you," he said. "For being there for Jon and Sutton today. And for sharing your time with me tonight."

"I...I need to go." Amber made fast her escape.

Paul remained on the bench a while longer. His thoughts were in disarray, tumbling over each other. But ultimately they returned to the scene he'd witnessed that afternoon: Amber running to Sutton and Jon and them throwing themselves into her arms...much the way they'd seek solace from a mother.

It seemed they, too, responded to the gentle spirit Amber Montgomery tried to keep hidden.

When Amber arrived at the camp kitchen the next morning, three messages tacked to the door awaited her. As she pulled them down, she wondered who'd gotten up before her. No one had stirred in her dorm or on the compound when she'd slipped out at four-thirty to get showered and dressed. She glanced at her watch. In a mere two hours a hungry throng crowding the dining hall would again trash her cooking.

But Amber—a fast learner in every regard except the one that mattered most—had already figured out how to forestall that backlash and whining: stick to the program. Instead of the stuffed French toast with strawberries and cream that she'd initially planned, she'd find something else. She reached for the binder and Jocelyn's breakfast menus.

She started a pot of coffee, then slit open the first message, folded over three times.

> *I loved the cream sauce and waffles yesterday. If, by chance you're going to whip up some adult food after you prepare the kids' meals, I'd love to get some.*

The note was signed *Harriet*.

Amber smiled. At least somebody appreciated her efforts.

She opened the next message.

> *Kirsten and Leanne told me about that great salad you made for lunch. Any leftovers available?*

It was signed *Nancy Baines*.

Laughing, Amber reached for the third missive.

Her breath caught and the smile fell from her face.

She stared at the words, hardly believing what she saw on the small sheet of paper.

* * *

When Caleb found himself at loose ends on Saturday morning he decided to work out a bit. His visits with Roy always left him in a funk that no amount of prayer or Bible study or meditation ever lifted. It almost seemed as if his brother sapped from him every ounce of energy he had in his body. Caleb didn't like visiting the prison, but he felt he owed Roy some kind of allegiance.

This last visit had proved otherwise.

Maybe.

If he followed through on what had been laid on his heart, he'd be spending a lot more time in jails and prisons. The thought didn't sit well with him.

Before the accident Roy had been a firm but fair man—at least, that's how Caleb knew his brother. The Roy that Marnie married, however, was a different man, a hard-drinking man who seemed to suck all of the life and joy out of her.

She'd blossomed in the time since Roy's conviction.

Caleb paused in the middle of a repetition with the free weights and gave that some thought. He'd heard whispers about Roy, about things he'd supposedly said and done. Cops talked like that. But who was he supposed to believe—his own flesh and blood or unsubstantiated rumors?

He put the weights down and headed to the locker room. The only place he wanted to be at the moment was with Marnie, and since she was up at Community

Christian's camp, that meant he couldn't sort of drop by Sunshine and Rainbows the way he tended to do during the week.

When his cell rang, Caleb was glad for the interruption. "Jenkins here."

"Hey, Caleb. How busy are you?"

"Depends on what you're calling about," he told Paul. "Do you need me to pull a shift?"

"Nope. I was wondering if you could run something up here for me."

"Where are you?"

"At Camp Spirit Fire."

A slow smile split Caleb's face. "Oh, yeah? What is it you need?"

Amber found Paul splitting wood for the campfire. She watched muscles bunch and flex under the white T-shirt he wore. He'd removed his pullover sweater for the task; it lay on a stump not far from the growing pile of wood. He hefted the ax and brought it down right in the center of a big chunk. The wood pieces fell to either side.

"If you keep looking at me like that, I'm liable to damage something."

Amber averted her eyes, embarrassed to have been caught. "I..." She quickly gathered her scrambled thoughts. "It's not every day you see somebody doing the lumberjack thing. Where'd you learn to do that?"

Paul grinned and wiped his brow with the back of his

forearm. "Manuel showed me about twenty minutes ago. Did you get my note?"

"I did. That's why I came up here. You shouldn't have said that."

"It's true."

Amber folded her arms. "True or not, you can't run around leaving notes like that on doors."

"I left one note, for one woman. So, will you?"

Amber blinked. Tried to get her bearings. Tried to understand what was behind his interest.

The note he'd tacked to the door for her that morning was an invitation. White-water rafting. With him. A sort-of date, by Amber's estimation.

Several teams were going out. Her kitchen duties were done. The midday meal consisted of bag lunches she and the girls had prepared right after breakfast. Everyone would be out doing sporting activities today. Some had opted for hiking, others were either rock-climbing or canoeing on the placid man-made lake. The more adventurous souls would attempt to tame the rapids.

She'd always wanted to try that, but hadn't had the nerve to throw herself into a hollowed-out log several years ago and go barreling down a river when Angeline and Ben tried to talk her into trying the sport in Honduras.

"I'm not a very good swimmer."

Paul smiled. "I am. You'll wear a life vest and we'll have a great time."

"What about Sutton and Jonathan?"

He set up another large block of wood to cut. Then he brought the ax down, splitting the block in two. "Sutton is on a hike and Jonathan is with the other boys, learning how to rappel."

"Isn't that dangerous?"

"I took a look at the wall. It's very sturdy. He'll be fine. So how about it? Will you go white-water rafting with me?"

Amber studied him. If she planned to get over her aversion to police anytime soon, she may as well start with Paul.

"Okay."

About an hour or so later she regretted that easy acquiescence.

The teams, all outfitted and ready to brave the rapids, stood around eagerly awaiting their turn to board the rafts. But Amber was having serious second thoughts. The boat looked too small and that water seemed awfully cold and deep.

It might be deceptively calm on the surface, but what lurked below and beyond? Amber identified with the water, cool and calm on the outside, with a churning, raging mass hiding beneath the depths. She stared at it as she waited to be called forward for her group's safety lesson and rafting demonstration.

"You ready?" Paul asked.

"I don't think so."

"You'll be fine," he assured her.

Marnie and four others completed their demonstration

and joined their river guide at their boat. With everybody strapped into life vests, they all looked to Amber like mini-blimps about to float above the Macy's Thanksgiving Day Parade.

"I don't know how to swim," she said when their river guide asked if anyone had any questions. "What if I fall in?"

"Falling in can be the best part," the enthusiastic guide said. When Amber frowned, he quickly added, "But that's why I'm here. And," he said, slapping Paul on the back, "you've got not only a life vest, but one of the best wild-river riders in the region right here."

"You've done this before?" she asked Paul.

He nodded.

"He's being modest," insisted the guide. "When we end our run, I'll tell you about a Class V river we've both run. Everybody ready?"

Amber settled into position in their raft and, without even realizing it, said a quick prayer.

"Hold on," the guide said. "Here we go!"

The raft barreled into the middle of the river. About one hundred yards out, they turned a bend and water sprayed up and around them. Amber let out a whoop that had Paul and the others laughing.

"Whoo-ee!"

The rush, glorious and liberating, pulsed through her like life-giving energy. "This is better than a roller coaster!" she hollered, enjoying the thirty-five minute ride.

Amber held her position, working the river with

gusto, wondering why she'd put off this great experience until now. Taking this wild ride was like nothing she'd ever done.

"Left, left!" Paul said, as the boat hurtled over a particularly rough patch.

"Easy now, everybody," the guide directed. "Easy. We're almost home."

The five river runners could see the end of the route. Waving, the others waited on shore to welcome them after the triumphant run. Amber, thinking about taking another ride down the river, took her attention off the water.

"Look out!" the guide yelled.

Out of nowhere, the rocks came at her. She'd taken her eyes off the river for a moment, just a moment. Amber lost her paddle and floundered, reaching for it. A rush of voices, everyone yelling. Then the tumble. And the water.

Shocking.

Cold.

Surrounding her.

"Help me, Lord. I can't swim. Help me, Lord."

❧ Chapter Twelve ❧

Icy fear clawed her insides, making her want to scream. But Amber knew how to deal with pain. And she knew not to cry out. That only brought more pain.

Things were somehow different this time.

He'd never tried to smother her.

Also different: This time she wanted to live. Not to cower or die like an abused animal. She wanted to live!

Strong arms clamped around her waist. She wouldn't let him win this time. She could fight. For herself. For her life.

The arms tightened, and Amber swung her arm out, aiming for any part of her attacker. She kicked and scraped and felt water rush down her throat.

Waves of blackness, of a forever nothing rippled through her.

He was taking her down, but Amber refused to go. She

kicked and broke the surface, sputtering and coughing, trying to take deep life-giving breaths.

And then the hands again, grasping at her. Tugging. Pulling at her hair. He was screaming her name.

This time the neighbors would surely hear. They'd come to her rescue. Surely.

But no one came to help. She slipped under again, looking for that peaceful place she sometimes found during the worst of it. Her lungs were filled with fire, heat pushing in all directions looking for an outlet.

Amber flailed. Refusing to give in.

Not again.

Not this time. If she died this time, at least she'd go out fighting.

Paul dove after her again. He'd had a good hold and had been kicking them to shore when she'd twisted and socked him with a punch that carried a wallop. She fought him like an alley cat, hampering his efforts to get her above the surface and pulled to shore. Though she wore a life vest, her panic could do her in.

The water wasn't that deep here, maybe seven or eight feet, but it wouldn't take that much to drown them both, the way Amber flailed about.

He wrapped his arms around her and kicked for the surface. They broke it, gasping.

"Here, man. I've got you." The river guide tugged on Paul, getting them closer to safety.

"No!" Amber screamed.

She lashed out, twisting with everything in her. Breath rushed from him and he couldn't hold on.

Paul saw the guide dive after her. Treading water, he shook his head, took a deep gulp of air and plunged under the surface again. This time, the current fought against him. There! A flash of blond hair. He shot his hand out, but came up empty. A moment later though...there!

He reached Amber at the same time as the guide. Together they hauled her, swimming for shore and the hands that reached out to pull them all out of the river.

Embarrassment quickly replaced fear. She felt vaguely silly having struggled against Paul, but Amber still didn't like the added attention, people scrutinizing her every breath. Not when she was dripping wet and looking like a drowned kitten. Her teeth chattered.

"Here, let me get another blanket to put around your shoulders," Paul said. He came back with a thermal survival blanket.

She looked at him, really looked at him. "Why are you being so nice to me?"

"You had a scare out there," he said. "I'm worried about you." Then, possibly sensing that there was more to her question, he paused mid-tuck. "I care about you, Amber—"

Her breath caught.

"I care about every person here," he finished.

She exhaled slowly. He spoke in generalizations, not specifics. Getting to know him in this setting was different, but the bottom line would always be that he was a cop. Doing a job. Some of them apparently took seriously their oaths to serve and protect. If serving meant rescuing a panicked woman in the middle of a domestic violence flashback while treading water in a raging river, so be it.

"Did I do that?"

He fingered his bandaged forehead, a cut near his eyebrow. "Yeah. But I'm okay."

A part of Amber wanted to apologize. But the words wouldn't come. She'd spent too many years apologizing for things that weren't her fault. The Anaheim Angels losing a game. Putting the wrong brand of mayo on Raymond's roast beef sandwich. The laundry service adding too much starch to his uniform.

Amber swallowed, then took a deep breath. Raymond Alvarez wasn't here. Paul Evans was the man with the bandage. The man who'd helped save her from drowning.

They were both cops. Cops with deep blue eyes. But Paul's eyes were different. There was warmth and concern in his. Not the ice and indifference she'd learned to recognize as the precursor of what would be a bad night in the apartment she shared with Raymond.

"Are you warm enough?"

She nodded.

"An ambulance is coming."

"I don't need an ambulance," Amber said. "I'm fine. Really."

"I'm worried about you, Amber. You took in a lot of water."

She tried a smile, but knew it looked pathetic. "I'm fine. Just a little cold."

She gathered the second blanket closer to her body. "When you worked in L.A. with the police..."

He glanced over at her, an air of expectancy in his expression, almost as if he held his breath awaiting her question.

"Did you know a Raymond Alvarez?"

He thought about it for a moment, then shook his head. "The name doesn't ring any bells. But the LAPD is huge, really huge. It's not anything like the Wayside Police Bureau where everybody knows everybody and their families, too."

Amber nodded. She was trying to get a handle on this man, on why, without even trying, he seemed to be breaking through all of the defenses she'd carefully erected over the past few years. The last thing she wanted in her life was another complication. Being friends with a cop—Caleb Jenkins excluded because she'd met him in a different setting—was not in the game plan.

Neither was hanging out at a church camp.

She didn't like the thoughts that lingered in her mind. Years ago when she still believed in redemption and devoting a lifetime of work to God, she never made a move without being sure of the next step, confident in her ability to distinguish God's will from her own. But those inner voices had been silenced. And Amber had no intention of heeding it at this point in her life.

"How many bad cops work in Los Angeles?"

Paul seemed surprised by the question. "I'd say a lot. A force the size of the one in L.A. has a percentage of cops who go bad. The sheer numbers account for that. But the majority of a police department's employees, here as well as there, choose this line of work because they come from cop families, or maybe they have something to prove to themselves. A lot of people become cops simply because they want to help people."

"Help them what?"

Paul chuckled. "It'll sound hokey, but the answer is, help people live in a just society. People should be confident that laws exist to shield society from anarchy. Law enforcement officers exist to shield the public—"

"Here's a cup of coffee, Amber," a teenager interrupted. "Maybe it'll warm you up."

"Thanks," she said, taking a sip from the paper cup. The teen went to check on the others who'd been in Amber's boat. "Isn't that a rather rose-colored view of the world?"

"What?" Paul asked. "That people simply obey the law?"

Amber shrugged. "Yeah. You know they aren't going to. Doesn't that make what you do," she shrugged again, adding, "pointless? Don't you ever get tired of going through the same motions over and over?"

"I'm sworn to protect and serve the public," he told

her. "I took a solemn oath in L.A. and one here in Wayside, giving my word that I'd lay down my life to protect the public. We each have callings on our lives. I've always known that mine was to uphold man's law in God's world."

Amber smirked, not buying or understanding that kind of commitment. "Yeah. Okay."

Paul folded his arms. "Is it the law part or the God part that you don't believe in?"

She looked up at him. Not liking the vantage point of him towering above her, she scrambled to her feet, shrugging off his assistance as the blanket fell from her shoulders.

Amber knew he waited for an answer, but the look in his eyes, something that seemed a hybrid of curiosity, pity and pique, irritated her.

She reached for and shrouded herself in the warmth of the survival blanket. She had to get away from him, away from those startling blue eyes that cut so sharp, those eyes that didn't miss a thing. From her own peripheral vision, she saw the river guide approach.

"Excuse me," she said.

"Hey, how ya doing?" the other man asked as he draped an arm around Amber's blanketed shoulders. "That was quite a tumble you took. How are you feeling?"

They walked off, leaving Paul standing there, his unanswered question hovering in the air like an abandoned child—or a lost dream.

He had other questions for Amber Montgomery. Like

what had happened to her in L.A.? And just who was Raymond Alvarez?

She'd fought him in the water, fought as if her very life depended on it. He'd seen the terror in her eyes. It wasn't fear of the water, even though she couldn't swim.

Tumbles from rafts weren't uncommon. Everyone else had laughed it off and waded to shore. Amber, though, she'd panicked, and in the process almost got them both killed.

What troubled Paul was the knowledge that it hadn't been the river that caused her distress. *He'd* been the cause of it. Somehow, and again.

"I'd like to talk with you about Amber Montgomery," Paul told Cliff later that day.

In his time in Wayside, Paul had come to count Cliff Baines as more than a pastor and a wise man; he considered the man a friend. And in this regard, he needed to speak to a friend.

"What about her?" Cliff asked. He closed the laptop and pushed it aside.

Cliff claimed a small room off the common lounge in the lodge as his office. While the kids cleaned up after their excursion, Paul found Cliff there. The pastor's camp study included a rough-hewn table that served as his desk. It was made of the same wood as the furniture in the lodge. A lamp, a file cabinet and a plaid love seat that had seen better days completed the room's decor. The only item that interrupted the rustic feel of the space

was a computer monitor and docking station for the laptop that at the moment lay on top of a file of manila fold-
ers.

Since the walls, covered with framed photos of
groups of campers, seemed to close in on Paul, he
stood, facing one of the pictures but not seeing anything in it.

"I was just wondering," he said as nonchalantly as he
could, "if there was anything I should know about her."

"Know? Like what?"

The minister wasn't making this easy. It would help,
Paul figured, if he had a better handle on just what it was
he was asking the preacher.

"We've had a couple of run-ins," he said. "She seems
to shut down. To disengage."

Cliff nodded. "That would be Amber. She pretty much
stays to herself, always has in the years I've known her.
You do know that she and Haley Brandon-Dumaine are
cousins."

Paul nodded. He'd gathered that from the cookout. "I
guess I just wondered if she was prickly around men in
general, or if it was just me."

Cliff raised an eyebrow. He settled back in his chair,
folded his hands over his stomach and tried to bite back
a small triumphant smile. "I thought you were interested
in Marnie Shepherd."

Paul faced the preacher. "I..." He paused. Then he
perched on the edge of the love seat. "I'll make no secret
of it, Pastor. It may sound old-fashioned, but I need a wife.

The Lord led me here not just for a job and a good place to raise my niece and nephew, but to find a spouse."

"We have an active singles ministry," Cliff said.

But Paul shook his head. "I'm not interested in parading women through my house or my life with Jon and Sutton. Stability is what I'm seeking."

"And you think you'll find it in Amber?"

"No," he said. "I'm not interested in her that way." But even as Paul said the words he wondered about their veracity. "Amber discounts faith. She doesn't want any part of any of the religious activities here or anywhere else."

Cliff sighed. "That's true."

"The woman I settle down with will have to love the Lord with all her heart and mind and spirit. I was just asking about Amber because of what happened today."

The minister sat up. "What happened today?"

Paul related the white-water rafting incident and Amber's response in the water.

Leaning forward, Cliff braced his elbows on the desktop and steepled his hands. "From what I know of Amber, and it's not a lot," he said, "she had a rough time before she arrived here in Wayside. Her parents live not far from here, but I don't think she has any contact with them."

"Why?"

Cliff shrugged. "What I do know is that Amber Montgomery, like everyone else including you, is here at Camp Spirit Fire for a reason. The Lord got her here via a need in the kitchen, but there's something else here for her. Maybe that something else is you."

Paul actually laughed at that. "I don't think so, Pastor. I don't believe in being unequally yoked."

"Hmm" was all Cliff said to that.

After the police chief left and Cliff returned to his notes for that evening's fireside message, he thought about Amber Montgomery. The woman was a dynamic cook, but she did have a troubled spirit.

He reached for his Bible and opened it to the third book of Proverbs. "In all thy ways acknowledge him and he shall direct your paths."

Cliff considered the Scripture for a moment, then opened the laptop and deleted the sermon he'd started. Tonight he'd speak about letting the river, like God's love, flow in its own direction.

"Hey, Marnie."

Caleb approached the table where Marnie was setting out craft supplies. Two plastic milk crates were filled with items soon to become works of art.

A smile blossomed across Marnie's face. "What are you doing here?"

"I had to bring the chief some paperwork, but I came with the ambulance."

She dropped a box of wooden craft sticks and rushed toward him. "Ambulance? What's wrong? What happened?"

"Whoa," Caleb said, steadying her with hands at her waist.

He brushed hair from her face and desperately tried not to think about how good it felt to hold her, even in this innocent way. Before his thoughts got out of control, he released her and bent to retrieve some of the wooden sticks that had fallen to the ground.

"False alarm. Again," he said.

"What happened?"

Caleb related what he knew of the struggle in the river.

"Amber must have been terrified."

He shrugged. "She's all right. Just a little shaken up was all. People get disoriented in the water."

Lost in thought, Marnie started placing the craft items at intervals on each of the picnic tables. Caleb watched her for a moment, then fell in and helped.

"And you said Chief Evans is the one who rescued her?"

"Yeah," Caleb said, peering into a box. "Are these bottles of paste supposed to go out, as well?"

"Two on each table."

Though Haley's matchmaking had a different goal, Marnie had seen what the others hadn't on the evening of the barbecue. Neither Amber nor Chief Evans realized that their gazes were constantly sliding off of each other. And after Amber's disappearing act, the police chief had gotten quiet, really quiet.

If Marnie had been in the market for companionship, she'd have been put out that night by the handsome police chief's obvious lack of interest. But since she'd walked the same path as Amber, Marnie knew the other woman could still be struggling with whatever had happened to her in Los Angeles. She offered up a prayer for guidance on how she could help Amber—and Paul—if need be.

"Marnie?"

She blinked. "Yes?"

"I was asking if you'd have dinner with me tonight."

She grinned at Caleb. "Sure. You really want to stay up here and hang out with a bunch of little kids?"

"It'll be fun," he said, giving her a smile in return. "I've never been to church camp."

"Well, this is a good day to visit," she said, turning back to the box of supplies. "It's the only night that Pastor Cliff actually delivers a message. Usually in the evenings after he or Nancy leads a short chat, we sit around the campfire singing, roasting marshmallows, that sort of thing."

"I wish my church did something like this."

"You can always join us at Community Christian."

Caleb put the last glue pot on a table, then gazed at Marnie. Had she been looking in his direction, she would have seen his heart in his eyes. "I'll give that some thought."

Paul's goal for the weekend was to give Sutton and Jonathan a bit of independence, to let them interact with other people without him constantly hovering nearby. Jonathan had yet to return from his morning excursion, and Sutton was in the dorm with the other girls, changing into messy clothes for arts and crafts.

With time to spare, Paul thought he'd take a walk around the camp, just to explore. He just hadn't bargained on having a follower dog his footsteps. Since returning from the white-water rafting excursion, he'd developed a shadow.

"I wanna be a policeman when I grow up," Max Young announced.

"I know that, Max."

The little boy's legs pumped hard to keep up with Paul's longer strides. Paul wasn't trying to ditch the child, he just felt compelled to check on Amber. A group of about seven teenagers sat under a tree talking. They waved as Paul and Max went by.

"Do you watch the police shows on TV?"

"Some of them."

"Jon says you're the best policeman ever. That you always catch bad guys. He said that you put bad men in jail for a long, long time."

That stopped Paul. His heart gave a little lurch. He paused and stooped down so he could look Max in the eye. "Does Jon talk about that a lot?"

The boy shrugged. "Sometimes. He told me that it's his job to watch out for his little sister. She has pretty hair."

Paul smiled. He ruffled Max's hair. "Yes, Sutton has pretty hair."

A car pulled into the drive and made its way up to the front of the lodge. The teens jumped up and ran over to greet the woman getting out.

"She has pretty hair, too," Max said.

Paul smiled down at Max, who was apparently a ladies' man in training. Looking up again, he recognized Kara Spencer. He'd met her once in town, and saw her occasionally at church, but hadn't spent any time with her. She was the psychologist that Amber had suggested he speak with about the kids.

In the beginning, Paul had resisted counseling, for himself or for the children. Then his captain had referred him to a group therapy program and his outlook had changed dramatically. There he'd met other men and women just like himself—cops who'd lost their loved ones to violence.

He'd learned the power of letting go of emotions that remained bottled up inside. He'd learned how to harness his anger and turn it into productive activity. And with a single-minded determination, he'd hunted down the people responsible for Mikey's and Sarah's brutal slayings and had seen them brought to justice.

The children rarely, if ever, talked about that time—at least, around him. The therapists said Sutton was too young to remember much of what actually happened that night. But her older brother's fear and descriptions fed her own, so much so that Paul had gotten help for both of them. But now, apparently, Jon had brought it up with his friend Max. Paul wondered if with the move to Wayside he'd done the right thing in removing them from all connections to their dead parents.

The counselor in L.A. advised that he just wait and see

how things went in Oregon. If the children showed any signs of mental distress or if anything happened to remind them of the trauma they'd suffered, time with a good therapist in Oregon would be in order.

"Hello there," Kara Spencer called out.

"Hey, Chief," Max said. "It's time for my class. I gotta go now, okay?"

Paul smiled at the boy. "All right, Max. I'll see you later."

Kara stuck out a hand as they watched Max scurry toward the tables where Marnie talked to his patrol sergeant. "I see you've made a new friend. You probably don't remember me. I'm Kara Spencer. Welcome to Wayside."

"I remember you, Dr. Kara."

She rolled her eyes. "Please, just Kara. Are you doing a workshop, too? Mine starts at three."

"Workshop?"

"I have two groups this time—our scholarship kids and the senior level counselors, mostly high school juniors and seniors. I'll bet your session will be jammed if you're talking about careers in law enforcement."

"So this afternoon is like career day?"

"Something like that." She hefted her satchel onto her shoulder and started walking toward the lodge. Paul fell into step beside her, much the way Max had done with him.

"I understand you're a therapist."

She nodded. "My practice has evolved over the years."

"You work with children primarily?"

Kara stopped walking. She faced him, giving him her full attention. "Not specifically or exclusively. Would you like a recommendation for someone in town or in Portland? You have what, a son and a daughter?"

"I'd just been giving it some thought."

"I'll jot down a couple of names for you."

"I'd appreciate it, Doc. Maybe we can talk before you leave today?"

Her steady gaze met his. "Sure, Chief."

Cliff Baines's hands hovered over the keyboard, not quite sure where to land. Trying to make sense of all the highlights he wanted to hit tonight didn't help one bit when the dominant image was a river, a fast-moving river.

Intellectually he knew that hearing about the white-water rafting incident was what had set the river image so firmly in his mind. But now he couldn't get his mind off of it.

"Like a tree planted by the river," he wrote.

The cursor blinked at him. Cliff stared at the words on the monitor, stared as if the answer to world peace had been laid on his doorstep. He realized he didn't need a prepared message to speak to his youth congregation gathered at Camp Spirit Fire. They came up here every year for friendship and fellowship, to get in touch with nature and to get a little closer to God.

He balled up the sheet of paper and made a jump shot into the trash can.

He didn't need notes for what he'd speak about tonight. He'd preach from the heart. But he might need a spiritual interpreter, someone who wanted to and didn't mind giving a testimony about the goodness of the Lord.

Cliff had just the person in mind.

❧ Chapter Thirteen ❧

The dispute started over a candy bar and who had first dibs on it.

"Give it back," Sarita yelled.

Her twin, Tanita, one of the girls who'd been involved in the earlier dispute, stood to the side. "Let it go, Ree. It ain't worth it."

"Yeah, listen to your sister, Ree-Ree," taunted the girl who'd snatched up the last chocolate bar, the very one that Sarita had been reaching for. Daphne ripped open the chocolate and took a big bite out of the bar.

Sarita swiped at the candy. But Daphne tossed it to a friend, who sneered at the twins before taking a bite herself. "And your shoes *do* have holes in them."

Daphne's friend tossed the bar to a boy who was standing nearby. The five, all eighth graders at Wayside Middle School, didn't get along in school and carried that bad blood with them throughout the summer and into the new school year.

Part of the church's outreach ministry, they and ten others were attending Community Christian's fall jamboree on scholarships.

Sarita lunged for the candy bar, but the boy, Kevin, took a bite and held the remaining portion high over his head.

Daphne and her friend laughed at the girl's effort to get the candy, and her sister's equally strong efforts to pull her away from the fray.

"Come on, Ree. Forget them. We came up here to have some fun, not mess around with knuckleheads."

"Who you calling a knucklehead?" Daphne said, pushing up into Tanita's face.

"You."

The shoving commenced.

"What's going on here?" Adam demanded, approaching the girls who were mere seconds away from physical blows. He looked at Tanita. "I thought we had a talk already today."

"I ain't doing nothing! You need to be talking to that thing over there."

Sarita shoved at her, but Adam intervened. "This might be how you settle disputes at home, but it isn't the Community Christian way."

Daphne jerked her arm free. "I didn't even want to be at this stupid camp—"

"Well, that can easily be remedied."

The thirteen-year-olds cast apprehensive eyes up at the big man who'd come over.

"Adam, I think our friends here would like a little education on what happens to young people who cause trouble here and in town."

Adam regarded the police chief with as much wariness as the squabbling middle schoolers who'd all grown quiet. "I'll set up a time with Mrs. Baines so you can have a group."

"Thanks," he said. Paul sent the five a not-quite-friendly smile, one reserved for recalcitrant prisoners who thought they'd gotten away with a jailhouse violation.

He met each teenager's eyes, then nodded at Adam and sauntered away.

"Just remember," Sarita said, "payback is a—"

Tanita tugged on her twin and whispered, "We at church, girl. Watch your mouth. Plus, you heard that cop."

Still angry and fussing under her breath, Sarita let her more levelheaded twin lead her away. She turned back, though, just in time to see Leslie give her the finger.

Tonight, Daphne mouthed, promising yet another altercation.

From the sidelines, Amber had watched the run-in and she had watched the way the police chief asserted his authority without diminishing Adam's. Paul walked a fine line. She wondered if he handled other aspects of his life with such aplomb.

While all of the other young people were headed toward the lodge, Amber saw one girl slip away, heading toward the hiking trails.

Curious, Amber followed her.

Marnie planned to use part of the time at the jamboree to slip away and think about the job offer in Coos Bay. But she found it difficult to get her thoughts settled enough to do anything except complete her volunteer work. She loved working with kids. That's why she'd accepted the position at Sunshine and Rainbows, and why she could always be counted on to put in at least one day of volunteer effort at the church camp.

But lately, Marnie had found her original inspiration for wanting to work with youth diminished.

She believed that each person was called to a certain work in the kingdom. But what she didn't know and couldn't assess is whether she'd embraced her own calling...or run from it.

A tug on the hem of her blouse drew her attention back to the moment.

"Mine doesn't look like yours."

Marnie smiled at the girl. Sutton Evans had blossomed in the past few weeks. Marnie had heard more words out of the girl in two weeks than she had in the previous three months. If anything, Marnie pinpointed it to the day Amber came to the center and Sutton was chosen as the Cookie Lady's helper.

"That's because art is individual. That's what makes it special. All of them are one-of-a-kind masterpieces."

Sutton studied her sticky mountain of wooden craft sticks and then a sample Marnie had placed on each table.

"It's supposed to be our church."

"And it's a fine church."

Sutton's lower lip trembled. She sat on the bench and blinked back tears.

"Sweetheart, it's okay. Every piece is supposed to be different."

"But I want my house to be perfect."

The words struck a chord with Marnie. She'd wanted her own house with Roy to be perfect. *From the mouths of babes,* she thought.

She wiped Sutton's eyes with a tissue and thought about shedding a few tears herself. "Would you like to start over?"

The little girl nodded.

Marnie placed the box of craft sticks within reach and handed Sutton two to start. Instead of immediately reaching for glue and other sticks, the child studied her first effort, looked at the sample and then sat there for a moment.

The child's concentration as she carefully considered her next move floored Marnie. It was as if a figurative lightbulb flashed over her head.

Instead of carefully considering her situation, Marnie had run headlong into the first opportunity to heal her wounded pride. Her husband hadn't valued her as a person, so she'd found the love and affirmation she craved in the smiles of children. Their messy artwork and sticky hands and big hearts soothed the ache fostered by Roy. Though she hadn't caused his accident or killed all those children, she bore the guilt as if she had.

So she found a niche in the day care center work. It was good work, honorable service, and to Marnie's thinking a form of payback, though small, for what Roy had done.

But she couldn't live her life trying to right Roy's wrongs. She enjoyed her life now. Now that Roy was locked up, paying penance for those deaths...and for abusing her all those years?

Marnie swallowed a lump in her throat.

Was it wrong to think that?

"I like this one better," Sutton said.

Marnie smiled at the girl. Sutton had a lot of words to share today.

Just like Sutton, she'd wanted her own house—her marriage—to be perfect. But when it didn't turn out the way she'd planned, instead of inspecting the base to ensure a sound foundation, she'd retreated.

At the time it had seemed the only option. But now she knew better.

Angela McReady hiked up to the bluff and looked out over the edge. It was a long way down, the terrain pocked by brush and trees growing out of the side of the mountain and between the jagged rocks.

The teenager sat on the ground and edged close to the rim. She kicked a few loose stones and listened to hear them land. No sound returned.

"It's pretty up here, isn't it."

Startled, Angela yelped, then scrambled back a few feet to relative safety. "Uh, yeah."

"Do you mind if I join you?"

The girl looked Amber over. Sensing no threat, she nodded.

Amber settled on the ground, crossing her legs and staring out at the horizon.

After several minutes passed and the young woman said nothing at all, Angela turned to her. "Well?"

Amber leaned back, her hands behind her, her face to the sun. "Well, what?"

"Aren't you going to start telling me about Jesus?"

Amber's laugh echoed around them. "Hardly. I'm not one of them. I'm just the cook."

"Your food wasn't so bad the other day. I kind of liked it."

Amber glanced at her. "Thanks."

And that was all that was said between them.

A bird circled overhead, then swooped down, somewhere below the promontory, in search of small prey. They sat there, listening to the sound of the day, letting the sun's rays warm them.

"Maybe this whole grant thing wasn't such a good idea," Kara said. She had about thirty minutes before she met with her group, and had caught up with Nancy in the lodge.

"Don't say that, Kara," Nancy told her. "If you hadn't written that grant proposal for us, we wouldn't have been able to reach out to so many children in the community. Yes, there have been a few problems and a couple of kids aren't adjusting so well, but there are always wrinkles to iron out during the jamboree. And it's just a weekend, after all." Nancy picked up a miniature box of raisins from a bowl on the table in the middle of the sofa grouping.

"Wrinkles we can handle. Kids who are constantly at each other's throats is something else altogether." Kara tucked her hands in her pockets and paced the area in front of the big fireplace. "I guess I'm just concerned that our kids, the members of Community Christian, will be influenced by the things they see the others doing and getting away with."

"No one's gotten away with anything," Nancy assured her. "And if any influencing is going on, I think it'll be the other way around."

She consulted her clipboard and flipped through several sheets. "I've already done some rearranging among the groups for the talent show. I separated the Jackson twins, as well as Daphne Gregory and her two pals. Instead of ganging up on each other, they'll be in different talent groups."

Kara nodded. "The teamwork should do them some good."

"I think so, too. By the way, Cliff, Adam and I met with the girls. And Adam says Chief Evans handled that last little squabble with finesse."

Kara smiled. "I'm sure Adam was more help than he realizes."

"You're probably right. We're really going to miss him when he heads off to college next year."

Nancy offered Kara the box of raisins. Accepting a few, Kara sat on the edge of one of the sofas and reached for her notebook. "Anything in particular you want me to focus on? I have the high schoolers."

"Nothing that I can think of. But if you have a moment and can find them, it might be a good idea to speak with Sutton and Jonathan Evans."

"The chief's kids?"

Nancy nodded. She told Kara what had transpired during the night and then that afternoon.

"I spoke with Chief Evans when I arrived." Something was going on with those kids. First Amber suggesting a chat with them, then the chief's not-so-subtle questions, now Nancy's comment. And if even Amber, someone who actively avoided anything that even hinted at traditional counseling, could recognize a problem, there must truly be an issue that needed to be addressed.

"Who has the group with the younger kids?"

Nancy smiled and waggled her fingers.

Kara grinned. "Well, that's convenient. What time would you like me to take your session?"

"You're sure?"

"It's not a problem." And it would give her an opportunity to meet the Evans kids.

"So, how's Marcus?" Nancy asked, after Kara scribbled the time and place into her notebook.

Kara's smile grew. "He's just fine. I heard from him this morning. He has two sold-out shows in Atlanta, then he's flying home."

"What's it like having a famous fiancé?"

Kara shrugged. "Since he's the only one I've ever had, I can't compare it to anything else. But guess what?"

"What?"

"Patrice is home for the weekend. And she said she'll make it up here tomorrow for the closing program. You should see her, Nancy. She is so jazzed about this whole record deal. That's what Marcus has to do when he gets back to L.A. There's some post-production work on her CD."

"Well, it's not every day a famous singer shows up in Wayside, sweeps off her feet one of our most beautiful and brightest, then drops a million-dollar record deal in her sister's lap."

Kara laughed. "You make it all sound so simple. The good Lord knows it wasn't."

Nancy winked. "But it was fun. You're in love and I'm very happy for you both."

Her answering smile told Kara's side of the story. She glanced at her watch and jumped up. "Gotta go."

"Have fun."

Twenty minutes later, Kara wondered if *fun* was the right word for the rap session. Instead of being energized like they usually were, the teens all seemed to be in a mood—a bad one.

"All right," she said. "We've been doing this for a while now. You guys know me. What's up? Why is everybody so mopey?"

Adam and Cindy glanced at each other, then glanced in Angela's direction. A few others shuffled their feet, looking at anything and everything except the quiet girl in the corner.

Kara remembered Angela. Her mother had died about a year ago. Cliff and Matt had asked if she'd do some counseling with her. They'd gotten together twice, and then Angela had simply stopped coming. Kara's efforts to find her were fruitless; it was as if she'd disappeared. And truth be told, with all the other craziness in her life, Kara hadn't followed through the way she would have liked to.

Kara nodded at Adam, then decided to try a different approach with the teen group. With luck, the activity might draw all of them out of their shells.

"I don't wanna sing any dumb old songs," Daphne announced to her team.

The assignments for the talent review had been announced during dinner. The teams had an hour or so to meet before the evening worship and campfire.

"We're just tossing out ideas right now," the captain said.

Each small group had seven members. The objective was to create a three- to five-minute sketch for presentation during the Sunday-afternoon closing program. To keep ringers and advance planning to a minimum, the teams were put together by the camp director, the head teen counselor—this year Adam Richardson—and one adult volunteer, all sworn to secrecy.

The teams had only the resources available to them at the camp to use for their skits, although some of the longtime campers had brought along in their luggage possible props, including clothing that could be converted into costumes.

"Well, if you don't like that idea, what suggestions do you have?" Max asked.

Daphne plopped into her chair and flipped the bill around on the baseball cap that covered her short red hair. "Here's a suggestion—how about if we all go home."

"You know," one of the older kids said, "your attitude this whole weekend has stunk."

Daphne swung her leg over the chair. "What's it to you? This whole place is dumb."

Cindy, the senior person in the room, decided it was time to intervene. "Let's go outside to talk, Daphne."

The recalcitrant teen rolled her eyes. "And what are you going to do, Little Mary Sunshine?"

"Don't pick on her!" one of the little girls said. "You're just being a bully."

Daphne jumped up, pushing her chair aside. It clattered to the floor behind her.

Suddenly, a wall of children faced her, all lined up in front of the little girl who'd called Daphne a bully.

"I think you should leave," Cindy said.

"Forget you," Daphne said, flinging at them the sheet with the team's rules printed on it. "Forget all of you Jesus freaks."

She clomped from the room, slamming the door behind her.

"I don't like her very much," Max said.

Cindy reached for the walkie-talkie and radioed Mrs. Baines. A few minutes later, the glum-looking group told Nancy and Paul what had happened.

"Do you know where she went?" Paul asked.

The team members shook their heads. "I hope she went home."

"Well, it's a long way to walk from here." He smiled at the children, giving them the reassurance they seemed to need. "Mrs. Baines, I'll look for her. Why don't you stay and get this group started on their skits."

"Chief Evans?" said Max.

"Yes."

"Do you need a description of the suspect?"

Paul tried hard not to laugh out loud. "I think we know what she looks like," he said. "But thanks for keeping your observation skills honed."

"Hey," someone said. "That's what our skit can be about."

"Yeah," another child said. "Max can be the investigator."

Paul snapped his fingers and pointed to Max. "See you later, Detective Young."

Max beamed at the praise from his hero.

Outside, Paul stood on the porch studying the layout of the camp.

Amber, carrying a large basket, approached. *Keep it light,* she coached herself. "Getting some air, Chief Evans?"

He smiled. "Call me Paul, please. And no," he said as Amber reached the porch. "So, are you Little Red Riding Hood?"

"Huh?" Then she looked at herself and chuckled. She'd donned a red windbreaker in case the evening turned cool before she finished her rounds. "Not quite. More like the Cookie Lady incognito."

He perked up at that and peered at the basket. "You have cookies in there?"

Amber laughed. "You're worse than the kids." But she reached in around the bags that had been packed to hold individual cookies and handed him two of her signature chocolate chip treats. "The kids here don't care for my cooking, but I know the cookies will be a hit."

Paul took a bite of one and moaned his delight. "This is almost enough to get my mind off the problem at hand."

"What's the problem?"

"If you were an angry thirteen-year-old girl who'd

just been run out of your youth group and you were essentially too far from home to walk, where would you go?"

"Well, first, when I was thirteen, the only place to hide was the back of a hut. Second, I was never in a youth group, so I don't know how I'd feel about being run out of one."

"Hypothetically, then."

"And the only place to hide is here?"

Paul nodded.

"Well, the bathroom, for one. I might just go to my bed or tent. But you know the best place I've found so far since I've been here?"

"What?"

"The boathouse. It's where they keep the canoes and fishing gear."

"Where is this boathouse?"

Amber pointed across the pond.

Paul finished off one cookie and started on the second one. "Too close and obvious," he said. "But I will check it out."

Amber glanced at him. He really was just a man. And as she watched his obvious enjoyment of her baking, a sense of pride and pleasure washed through her.

Then, before she chickened out, she said, "Would you like some company? On your search, I mean? You probably shouldn't go traipsing through the girls' dorm or tents by yourself."

"You're on."

She held the basket up. "I need to get these late-night treats to all the sites. It'll only take a minute."

"I'll be right here waiting."

He eyed the basket with a longing that tickled Amber. "Here, you big baby." She handed him two more cookies.

Paul grinned and bit into one. "Thanks."

It wasn't until Amber returned with the empty basket and placed it on a low table inside the lodge, that it dawned on Paul. He'd been the one to get the cookies this time.

So there, Caleb, he thought to himself. Then, he looked at the pretty blonde beside him, aware for the first time that his feelings had indeed changed where she was concerned.

He couldn't deny the fact to himself anymore.

He was interested in Amber Montgomery. Not so much in her past anymore. Just very, very...interested.

❦ Chapter Fourteen ❦

They searched all of the obvious places and a few not-so-obvious ones. Then, concerned that maybe the girl had indeed decided to walk home, Paul told Cliff that he was going to drive along the direct route to see if he could find Daphne or someone who may have seen her.

"Need a navigator?" the minister asked.

"Nope. I've put myself in the patrol shift since I've been here, so I know much of the town and surrounding area. I'll alert the on-duty units to be on the lookout, just in case."

"I guess I'll leave now."

Paul looked at Amber. He held her gaze until Cliff cleared his throat. "Uh, thanks for your help, Amber."

The three shared an awkward little moment, then Paul headed out. Amber got up to leave.

"Can I have a word with you?" Cliff asked.

She sat back down. "Sure. What's up?"

"I've heard nothing but rave reviews about your cooking."

Amber pursed her lips. "You obviously haven't talked to any of the kids at this camp."

"Not from the kids, from the adults. I understand you've been making dual meals. Camp grub for the youth, and serious food for the grown-ups."

Amber shifted in her seat. "Uh, well, I can pay you back if I used too much of your rations."

"No, no, no," Cliff said, coming around the desk and perching a hip on the edge. "I'm just wondering why no one invited me."

Still chuckling about Pastor Cliff, Amber thought about her mother's words: *"A hardworking man will serve up a hard-eating appetite."*

The smile fell from her face slowly as she made her way to the kitchen. She'd thought more about her parents in the past three days than she had in the past year.

She remembered one of the sermons her father had delivered on the mission field. They were in the compound where Ben and Angeline lived. In the soothing tenor that had lulled her to sleep on many a night, he'd sung a hymn about grace, then preached from John 10:10 about abundant life. "The thief comes to kill, steal and destroy, but I come that you might have life more abundantly." Amazingly, she remembered the verse, too. Maybe not word for word, but the essence of it.

With a song in his heart and a smile in his voice, her dad had held his Bible high, exhorting the villagers to embrace the love and peace of the Good Shepherd. In that moment, she'd loved the Lord more than ever, had rededicated her own life to Christ and vowed that she would walk in her parents' footsteps as an ambassador for the Lord.

Now Amber snorted. "Yeah, right."

But her derision faded in the face of what she'd seen so far at Community Christian Church's camp. Weren't they doing the same thing, except the mission field here was a domestic one instead of a remote overseas one?

She pulled out the key to the mess hall as she approached. Her father's sermon wasn't the only element she recalled of that long-ago night. It was the first time Ben had ever kissed her. Not full on the lips the way she'd seen some of the village couples kiss, but on the cheek, nice and sweet.

She smiled, remembering the gentle boy who, along with his sister, befriended a lonely little American girl. She missed Ben so much. Some of the grief she'd felt the night he died came back to haunt her now. He'd died trying to save not just any old dog, but the puppy she'd adopted.

Swallowing hard, Amber stuck the key in the mess hall door, but it swung open.

Her entire attention riveted to the door. It definitely had been locked.

She glanced around, suddenly wishing Paul was around.

She stepped into the mess hall and quickly flicked the switch near the door. The room suddenly flooded with light. And there, at a table near the kitchen, sat the missing Daphne, a five-gallon container of ice cream in front of her.

Amber and the teenager stared at each other for a moment, neither saying anything. Then Amber made her way to the table where Daphne sat. She didn't ask any of the obvious questions, the ones grown-ups always used to make her answer.

As a matter of fact, Amber didn't speak. Still holding the girl's gaze, Amber went to the racks holding flatware. She pulled out a tablespoon and returned to the table.

She peered into the container. "Neapolitan. I like strawberry." She stuck her spoon in and scooped up some ice cream. "Mmm, this is good."

Daphne just stared at her. "What are you doing?"

"Eating some ice cream."

"Why?"

"Because it tastes good," Amber said.

Daphne gave her a cross-eyed look. "What's with you?"

"What do you mean?"

"Aren't you going to ask me how I got in here?"

"Nope." Amber licked her lips, then stuck her spoon in for another spoonful, this time chocolate. "Want some strawberry?"

"How come?"

Amber glanced at her. "Because the strawberry is just as yummy as the others."

Daphne expelled a breath that made the freckles across her nose more pronounced. "How come you're not gonna ask me how I got in here or what I'm doing?"

"Duh," Amber said. "It's pretty obvious. You broke in the front door, went to the freezer and got some ice cream. Eating ice cream always helps me when I have things on my mind, too."

"What makes you think I have things on my mind?"

Amber just gave her a look.

"So, now what?" the girl asked.

"Now what, what?"

Daphne narrowed her eyes at Amber. "You're making fun of me."

"How am I doing that?"

She jumped up, fists balled, ready to brawl. "By... By... I don't know how. But you did."

"I was scared the first time I went to a church camp. Not here, of course—somewhere else. I didn't know anybody, didn't know how to make friends. I was miserable for days. And then something happened."

"What happened?"

"I had a bowl of ice cream with a girl at the camp. Well, not ice cream exactly, but the closest thing they had to it. This camp was pretty far away. Her name was Angeline."

Daphne reached for her spoon and scooped a generous portion of strawberry ice cream. "What'd you and this Angeline talk about?"

Amber shrugged. "Girl stuff. Not fitting in with the others. Boys and whether any of them would ever like us. You know, just talking."

"Uh-huh." Daphne settled in her chair again. "There's nobody to talk to here. They all think they're better than everybody else."

"Maybe. Sometimes other people are just as scared as you and me. They just hide it differently."

"I don't like to sing songs."

"So don't."

Not at all sure what to make of this odd adult, Daphne just stared for a full minute. "You make it sound so easy."

"It is easy," Amber said. "Do what you want to do. But realize you have to take responsibility for your actions. There are consequences for everything."

The wariness returned. "Whaddya mean 'consequences'?"

"Well, here's an example," Amber said, and she stuck her spoon into the ice cream container for another taste. "We're sitting here eating this good ice cream, right?"

Daphne nodded and helped herself to some more chocolate.

"But we're eating it straight out of the container that was for everybody."

"So?"

"So that means when we're done, we either have to have eaten it all, or the rest gets thrown away."

"We can't eat this much ice cream."

"Sanitary rules," Amber said. "Since we can't use this

container for the ice cream social tomorrow, that means one of two things."

"What?"

"I'll have to see if I can get another five-gallon bin, or we don't have enough ice cream for everybody."

"So get another one."

"I'll have to pay for it, probably out of my own money."

Daphne looked at her. "Your money?"

Amber nodded. "I'm responsible for the kitchen and all the meals here. Since something happened on my watch, I have to deal with it." She wasn't exactly sure if that was the case, but she'd have to find out. "The only other option would be to tell people we ran out."

"You could pretend like you didn't know what happened to the ice cream."

"True," Amber conceded. "But we'd both know. And that's one of the seven deadlies."

"Deadlies?"

"You know, the seven things God *really* doesn't like."

Daphne looked up, as if she expected something to happen to her for lying. "That other lady said there were ten rules."

Amber nodded. "That's a different list."

Daphne put her spoon down. "This isn't as much fun as I thought it'd be."

"The ice cream or the jamboree?"

"Both." She pushed her chair back. "I gotta go."

Amber licked the remaining ice cream on her spoon. "Okay."

"Are you gonna rat on me?"

Amber met the girl's hostile glare. "What do you think?"

"What do you mean, he's gone?" Sutton asked Jonathan. "Daddy wouldn't just leave us."

"The truck is gone," Jonathan pointed out.

Sutton chewed on that for a bit. "Maybe he went to the store."

"You stick by me," Jon told her.

"Okay." Sutton put her hand in her older brother's. Together they followed Cindy to the evening worship area. Jonathan assessed the seating options. "If we sit right here we can't see the road."

"I wanna see."

"Okay." He led her to a spot where they could see both the road and Pastor Cliff.

"You guys doing all right?" Cindy asked.

Jonathan nodded. Sutton looked at the ground. Other children filed in beside them.

Nancy made a few announcements before Cliff got up to speak. She consulted her ever-present clipboard, then beamed out at the group.

"Just a reminder, everyone, breakfast is at nine tomorrow. We start a little later because some teams like to get in an early morning practice. There'll be a meeting for all adult volunteers who can attend at eight o'clock in the dining hall."

Her smile encompassed everyone, from the youngest child to the seasoned veterans. "Anyone have any questions?"

A couple of hands shot up. After answering a question about the closing time, and assuring Max that, yes, he'd still have a chance to try the rock wall, Nancy glanced at Cliff.

"Well, as Pastor Cliff comes up, I have one more announcement," she said.

"Uh-oh," Cliff said. "That sounds like a setup. What'd I do now?" Cliff took his wife's hand in his.

Several people chuckled at the byplay between the two.

Amber, watching from the sidelines, marveled again at how open and easy their relationship appeared.

"It's not about you," Nancy assured him. "We'll have a special guest tomorrow for our closing. Some of you know Patrice Spencer from our concert after the film and music festival. Well, she's back home in Wayside now. She just finished recording her first gospel music CD. We're all very excited for her. She and Reverend Matt will give us a soul-stirring send-off to our fall jamboree."

Whoops followed that announcement. Cliff kissed Nancy, then took center stage.

"Well, my wife is always a hard act to follow," he said. "At least I wasn't in trouble this time."

"You're never in trouble, Pastor," somebody yelled out.

"Tell that to the boss," he said, indicating Nancy, who'd settled next to the Jackson twins.

Amber saw Daphne slink into an open space in the back. The girl didn't look happy, but at least she was there—

"Hey."

Amber jumped, her hand clutching her throat. "You scared me to death."

Paul grinned. Amber realized just how much she liked seeing him smile. When Paul Evans smiled, so did his eyes. Unlike her ex's, Paul's eyes held gentleness and warmth.

Spying him, Sutton waved furiously from where she and Jonathan sat near Cindy. Paul waved back.

"Want to come join us?" he asked.

Amber shook her head. "I'm not going to stay long. You go ahead. Looks like Sutton's saved a place for you."

"I'll see you later, then?"

His gaze connected with hers, and Amber's heart raced. The words, innocent enough, seemed to carry another message altogether. His eyes, a clear blue like a summer day or a chambray shirt, held no malice, no hidden agenda.

So was she hearing things, inferring inflection where none existed?

He reached for her hand and squeezed it gently. Then he turned away.

She watched him walk toward the place where Sutton and Jonathan waited. Even his walk was confident, his steps sure. Raymond had walked with a swagger, a calculated movement meant to convey his position and to intimidate both friend and foe. Paul, on the other hand, walked like a man with nothing to hide. Amber blinked back sudden tears.

"Way too much thinking and remembering this week-end," she muttered.

Tuning in to what Pastor Cliff was saying rather than where her thoughts led, Amber folded her arms and leaned against the tree trunk.

"As I was preparing my notes for tonight's message I realized that it wasn't a sermon I needed to preach this evening," the minister said. "I thought I'd start by telling you a story."

Cliff faced the campers, counselors, parents and volunteers. "We've been coming up here for several years, and each fall when we arrive for the youth jamboree, I'm struck by the beauty of the area. When we're at home, we don't often pause to appreciate the things that God put on this earth for us to enjoy. And here, where the air is clean, the water clear and where we fellowship in fun and friendliness, we have the opportunity not only to challenge our bodies—I have a couple of scrapes to prove just how much," he added, showing off his hands and elbows. "But to get closer to God."

Not in the mood for a quasi-sermon, Amber turned to leave.

"We had some people run the river today," said the pastor. "And I understand one of the boats took a tumble. Everyone's okay, but when I was told about that, it reminded me of just how much we depend on God."

Amber paused, wondering where he might be headed with his comments about her fall and near drowning. She leaned back against the tree, and could see Paul a few yards away. Sutton was in his lap, Jonathan at his father's right side.

"Sometimes in life we have to stumble, to fall. Maybe we rock the boat a little or even a lot. And sometimes we fall overboard. Without a life preserver."

Several people chuckled at that.

"But our help, even then, comes from the Lord," Cliff said. "Close your eyes for a moment and think about the worst day or time of your life. Bring it to the forefront of your thoughts."

Amber swallowed hard. She didn't close her eyes because she didn't want to think about that day, the worst one ever. As a matter of fact, she'd spent a lot of energy and time trying to banish it from her memory.

She watched Cliff Baines walk among his camp congregation.

"I know it hurts," he said. "Were you crying on that day or during that time? Did it seem like no one, not even God, could understand your problems, let alone help you?"

Amber saw several heads nodding. She folded her arms and quickly blinked back the moisture that had somehow found its way to her eyes.

"Take the hand of the person sitting next to you," the pastor said.

Amber wanted to leave, to run like she'd never run before. To run like she'd run *that* night. But her feet were planted to the ground. *"Like a tree, planted by the water."* The line rushed through her head, a forgotten vestige of her former life, and her former faith.

"Even with your eyes closed you can feel the person's hand in yours, can't you?" Cliff said.

Amber started.

Pastor Cliff was standing right there beside her. She hadn't even heard his approach, but now his hand took hold of hers.

"Jesus loves you," Cliff said.

Though his voice carried over all of the assembly, it seemed to Amber that he spoke the words quietly in her ear, only for her edification.

"He was there for you during that worst time ever and he's here for you now. All you have to do is open your heart and let him in."

"It's not that easy," Amber said, her face contorting. "It's not that easy." She wrenched her hand from Cliff's and stumbled away.

Paul heard her cry out, and turned in time to see Amber rushing away. He looked to Cindy to ask her to watch the children, but he saw Kara Spencer and Nancy Baines get up and follow Amber.

"Daddy, why are people crying?"

He hugged Sutton close. "Because sometimes they have burdens too heavy to carry."

"And crying makes it better?"

"No, pumpkin. Jesus makes it better."

∞ *Chapter Fifteen* ∞

It was late, close to eleven. The evening snacks had been consumed, the late-night talent-show rehearsals were over. Lights had gone out in the dorms almost an hour ago, but Amber, still keyed up, couldn't sleep.

Every time she closed her eyes, it seemed as if a wall of water crushed in around her, stealing her oxygen and her orientation. Is that what a near-death experience was like? This sense of stepping a safe distance away from the abyss.

She pulled a pair of sweatpants over her pajamas and tugged a Wayside College sweatshirt over her head. She hadn't been running in all the days she'd been at the jamboree. Edgy and irritable served as good descriptions of how she'd been feeling the past few days.

For a moment, Amber allowed herself to indulge in self-pity. But the party didn't last long. That was one of the things she'd learned in that counseling session, the one that ended with Amber getting a two-year-old headache. Maybe her body was just sending a message that it didn't like going cold-turkey off its regular exercise regimen.

She could run down to the camp road and maybe up the highway a bit. That might make two miles. She figured she could run it twice.

She stuffed into her pockets a compass and her driver's license, then snatched up the red windbreaker and headed outside.

But instead of heading toward the road, her feet seemed to move in another direction. Too tired to argue or to even consider that she again heeded not her own desires but some higher prompting, she just walked to the lake and sat on the ground, her legs crossed, the lake surface a mirror to her stillness. She sat that way for a long time, for so long that her legs cramped, for so long that a chill in the air made her shiver.

That's when she realized she wasn't alone—physically or spiritually.

"How long have you been standing there?" she asked him.

"Long enough to know not to disturb someone who is meditating."

"What makes you think I was meditating?"

He stepped toward her. "Where I come from, people who stare into a river are generally meditating, praying or doing some sort of ritual sacrifice."

She wrinkled her nose. "Where are you from?"

"Cajun country," he said. "I was born in Louisiana, but my parents moved to California when I was ten."

"Haley's husband is from Louisiana. He grew up there."

Paul smiled and shrugged. "I've been a few places, but not east or south. I may have been born in the South, but I'm Southern-California raised, and sometimes it shows."

"What's wrong with Southern California?"

"Why don't you tell me," he said. "You don't seem to like L.A. very much. Each time it comes up, you get tense."

Amber turned back to the still water, willing her shoulders to relax, disturbed that she had a reaction to Los Angeles that showed. "I prefer small towns."

"I'm finding I do, too."

"I don't understand you."

He held his arms wide. "What's to understand? I'm pretty open. I see things in black and white. There's very little gray area for me."

"Then, you miss a lot," she said.

"Why do you always fight me, Amber?"

"I don't know what you're talking about."

The response, instinctive and defensive, made Amber feel small. "I don't mean to," she told him. She shrugged. "I think I'm just not used to cops being genuinely nice."

"I'm more than a cop, Amber. I'm a man, first. Do you mind if I join you?"

She started to say something smart in response, then

just edged over, inviting him to sit without actually putting voice to the invitation.

"It's beautiful up here," he said. "It makes you forget that there's a world beyond the rising and setting of the sun."

"Are you a closet poet?"

He shook his head. "Nope. I've just learned how to appreciate natural beauty."

But as he said the words, his gaze lingered on Amber, not on the dark lake that shimmered quietly in the moonlight and on the surrounding trees.

"You know," she said, "in one of the places where I grew up, if a man and a woman talked together at the riverside, it meant they were agreeing to court."

"Hmm, maybe I should visit that place where you grew up."

"You wouldn't like it," she said. "Southern California is an asphalt jungle. The places where I was raised were just jungle, period."

But what he'd said—and the implications of that—sunk in a moment later. Amber looked at him then, really looked at him. "What were you saying, Paul? Just then, I mean?"

He reached for her hand, covered it in his much larger one. His hands were like the rest of him. Warm, comforting. Amber didn't pull away, and this time she didn't mind him holding her hand. It felt good. The way she supposed a normal woman felt when a man she liked held her hand.

A man she liked!

Amber's eyes widened and she snatched her hand away from him. Who was this man and why was he making her feel things?

"It means that I'm interested in you, Amber Montgomery. I've tried not to be."

"Gee, thanks. You really know how to flatter a girl."

"I think you know what I mean," he said. "There's something between us. Something that's been there from the moment we met."

"Well, let me tell you this," Amber said. "If your idea of wooing me is bringing up that night when you had me handcuffed and arrested, your approach needs some work."

"I'm sorry about that night, Amber."

She got up and skipped a pebble out along the smooth lake surface. It bounced several times as it skimmed along, then eventually sank.

"You're very good at that."

"I spent a lot of time at the riverside waiting," she said. "Waiting for someone to come join me."

"And how many times did that happen?"

"Once," she said. She turned to him. "Just now."

His gaze met hers, then dipped to her mouth. "I'd like to kiss you, Amber Montgomery."

He reached for her hand again and waited for her response. But Amber just continued to stand there, her gaze focused on something he couldn't see.

She didn't pull her hand away this time, but he felt her retreat.

"I'm not good at this," she said.

"Good at what?"

"Intimacy. Quiet moments with the opposite sex. There's something you need to know about me. I'm sure it will color the way you think you feel."

"We all have pasts."

She shook her head. "It's not that— Well, it is that. You're a police chief and I'm..."

"You're a beautiful woman who intrigues this single dad and cop."

"You sound like a personals ad." She tugged her hand away from him and got up.

Paul watched her. "That's it, isn't it. The kids? I'm a package deal, Amber."

"It's not your children. Sutton and Jon are wonderful. As a matter of fact, they're about the only kids I really understand."

"Let me help you."

She faced him, taking umbrage at the notion that a woman needed a man to rescue her. In Amber's experience, it was just the opposite. Women needed to be rescued *from* men.

"Excuse me? Help me? What makes you think I need help?"

He stood, too, tried to take her hand. "It's an educated guess."

Amber's own fear of the conversation and where it might be leading, what he might want of her, made her reckless. Instead of taking his words for what they were, she lashed out angrily. "I see the way you are with your kids, *Chief Evans*. I'm not a child. I don't need to be protected and shielded from the big bad world." She poked a finger in his chest. "I'm some kind of experiment for you, is that it?"

"What are you talking about?"

"I'm not something you can put under a microscope and study to see how I respond to different stimuli. I'm a living and breathing woman."

Everything had been going along fine, just fine. And then, just like Raymond used to do, Paul pointed out her flaws—all the things that needed fixing. By him. He reached for her, but Amber pulled away. "I have feelings," she said, tears starting to mix in with the words. "Feelings that nobody cares about."

She'd been trying to separate them. She knew intellectually that the blue-eyed cop who beat up on her wasn't the same blue-eyed police chief she'd been getting to know this weekend. But with what Paul said, the edges were starting to blur again.

"Amber?"

He reached a hand out to her, to steady her, but Amber was too worked up to see the danger of the large rock behind her. When he approached, she stepped back.

"Amber, look out!"

But too late, she stumbled over the rock.

Quick on his feet, Paul caught her before she fell, hit her head or landed in the lake.

They tumbled to the ground, Paul taking the brunt of

the fall. For a moment, Amber lay sprawled over him. Then she shuddered and scrambled away.

He knew Amber had nothing to fear from him.

The look in her eyes, however, said she believed otherwise.

"Amber?"

She'd curled into a ball, her hands shielding her face. "I'm sorry. I didn't mean to run away from you. Please don't hurt me."

Paul cursed himself a thousand times the fool. Suddenly it all made sense. The way she'd gone limp that first night, and then her attempts to fight for herself. The wavering bravado that was probably the only defense mechanism she claimed.

And he remembered the bruise he'd accidentally left on her arm the night they'd met. The way she'd lashed out at him in the water...

How could he have been so blind? The signs were all there. He'd been trained to watch for them. Yet, with this fragile woman, one he cared for like no other, he'd been oblivious to the pain that *he* caused her.

Amber wasn't a fugitive from justice or a woman on the run or one of the legion who just didn't like cops. She'd been abused by someone. Probably someone who looked or acted a lot like he did.

Other pieces of the puzzle fell into place then. Her reaction when she'd found out he'd been with the LAPD. Later, her questions about a specific L.A. cop. He groaned, realizing too late what all the pieces meant.

"Oh, Amber. I'm so sorry." He reached for her, to comfort her, but he stayed his hand.

Lord, give me the words. Guide my hands and my heart.

"Amber, it's me. Paul Evans." Despite the rage he felt toward the man who'd turned her into a woman living in fear, Paul kept his voice low, soothing. And he didn't touch her.

"I'm not going to hurt you. Can you hear me, Amber? It's Paul."

He looked around for help, but they remained alone at the lake. Nothing but the night surrounded them. He wanted to hold her, to tell her it would all be okay, but he didn't want to frighten her any more.

I need some help, Lord. Please.

Nancy and Cliff Baines sat up talking. Usually they slept apart during the fall camping trip because they were needed as chaperones in the dorms or tent sites. But this year, they'd had more than enough volunteers—too many, really. But at least each child got individual attention.

"I've noticed an interesting dynamic this weekend," Cliff said.

"What's that?" Nancy massaged her husband's shoulders as they talked.

"Have you looked at Paul Evans and Amber?"

"What do you mean, looked at them? I see them. Chief Evans decided to stay here after his children got spooked that first night."

"Not that. I mean the way they look at each other when they think no one's watching."

Nancy leaned over his shoulder. "Are you still playing matchmaker?"

"Me?"

The innocent question brought a smile to Nancy's face. "Yes, you, dear sweet husband of mine." She kissed his cheek.

Cliff turned his head and captured a real kiss before Nancy went back to kneading the muscles along his shoulders and back.

A moment later they switched positions and he worked the kinks out of her neck, shoulders and back.

"This is different," Cliff said. "Not like Haley and Matt, where everybody except the two of them could see they were made for each other."

"What, then?"

"I don't know. I do know Amber has a wounded spirit."

"Were you talking to her tonight?"

Cliff nodded. "I hadn't planned to. I was going to call on Kara to give her testimony, but something led me to Amber Montgomery instead. She's been on my mind and spirit the entire weekend."

"Mine, too. I've kept her in prayer, but I've been so busy putting out fires that I haven't had a chance to talk to her. *Really* talk to her."

"She's a very private person."

Nancy nodded. "And the police chief is very public,

very open. He loves those kids to distraction. But I'm worried about them, too."

"I talked to the Jackson twins after the service tonight."

"And?"

"And I think we won't have any more trouble out of them. As a matter of fact, Sarita wants to join the church," Cliff said. "She said she didn't come forward during the invitation tonight because she didn't want people to make fun of her, Daphne in particular." Cliff sighed. "Ah, young Miss Gregory. What other mischief has she been up to? Besides having Chief Evans out searching for her?"

"Nothing else that I know of, thank the Lord," Nancy said. "Everywhere that child goes, trouble is close behind. She eventually showed up, but didn't say where she'd been."

"Who spoke with her?"

"I did, but she'd never look me in the eye. So the Lord only knows what she'd been up to."

He expelled another breath. "Maybe next year we should screen the scholarship applicants a little better."

"Don't be discouraged," Nancy said. "This is just the first year of opening the camp to people who aren't members of Community Christian. Just because we have a few problems with a couple of kids isn't reason to shut down the whole program. Besides," she added, "this weekend may be their only exposure to the Gospel."

Cliff took her hand. "Have I told you lately how much I love you?"

Nancy smiled. "Yes, but I always like hearing it again."

"I love you, Nancy Baines."

"I love you, too, Pastor Cliff."

"I think there's some work that needs to be done. Join me?"

"Always," she said as she bowed her head, her fingers entwined with her husband's.

Cliff then began an intercessory prayer, lifting up all of the participants at Camp Spirit Fire, in particular the small group of young people, Amber Montgomery included, who still weighed heavily on his heart.

"Father God, we thank you this evening—"

A scream rent the night air, shattering the illusion of safety at the church camp.

It was a girl's long, terrified scream for help.

Chapter Sixteen

Paul's head whipped up at the sound of a woman's cry.

"What now?" he exclaimed.

A thought raced through his mind. Sutton? But the voice was too mature to belong to his daughter.

The cop in him wanted to secure the other location, but the man in him knew that other people were there to handle whatever that situation might be. He couldn't leave Amber, not the way she was at the moment, curled up, crying and shaking, locked in a nightmare and terrified of him.

His place, for now, was at the side of this woman who hurt so very much.

"Amber?" He touched her shoulder, lightly. "Amber, you're safe with me," he said.

Even as he said the words, he wondered how many times Amber and women just like her heard those words from their tormentors, from fathers, brothers, boyfriends, pastors and deacons. How many remained locked in an abused state of mind long after the physical torment ended?

He stroked Amber's back, trying to get a handle on what to say and do, since divine providence didn't seem to be raining down on him.

Or was it?

Paul sat on the ground, pulled her into his arms and rocked her until her cries became whimpers, until her whimpers turned to hiccups, and until she turned her wide-eyed but clear gaze directly on him.

She sniffled and ran a hand over her nose. "I'm sorry."

"There's nothing to apologize for."

"I didn't mean to... I mean, I'm sorry you had to witness that. I... Sometimes I forget and it seems like..."

She tried to pull away. Paul offered no resistance.

"You didn't hit me."

Taken aback at her incredulity, he just shook his head. "I don't hit women, Amber. I never have and never will."

Amber said, "I just thought, well, because of, you know...your..."

She blushed furiously. Sitting there with her in the moonlight, Paul found it enchanting that she could blush, given everything she'd been through and the state she'd been in just a few moments ago.

"Whenever Raymond, my old boyfriend, got aroused he used to..."

Fury radiated through Paul at the man who'd so carelessly used this fragile woman, but he held it in for Amber's sake—for his own sake.

"Real men don't beat up on women or anyone else," he said. "And they know how to control their urges."

Amber frowned. "What's that noise?"

Paul glanced back at the dorms where lights were now blazing and kids spilled out on the porches, everyone talking at once. "Something's going on at the camp."

"At—" Amber glanced at her wrist, then remembered she hadn't put her watch on for her run. "What time is it?"

"After midnight, I think," Paul said. "There are plenty of people who can handle what's going on over there. I'm concerned about what's going on right here."

She pushed completely away from him then. "Part of me thinks I owe you an explanation. The other part says, run as fast as you can."

He waited for her decision.

"I..." She glanced toward the main camp compound. "Maybe you're needed back there."

"I'm needed here more," he said quietly.

She rewarded him with a tentative smile. "Thank you."

In that moment, Paul knew that all the things he'd sought were right here in front of him. Not necessarily in the package he'd hoped to receive, but presented to him nonetheless as a gift from God.

Few, if any, gray areas existed for him. People were either law-abiders or law-breakers, believers or unbelievers, honest or dishonest. So it surprised him that when it came to Amber, he realized a gray area did exist. Amber lived in it.

From what she'd told him so far, Amber at one time had had a very deep and abiding devotion to the Lord. The circumstances of her life had changed that outlook, but maybe the reason she was brought here to Camp Spirit Fire this weekend was to reclaim the faith she had once known.

As if her thoughts were attuned to his, she said, "For a while, I grew up wanting to be a missionary like my parents. Then I discovered the true value of an American dollar, and I never wanted to go back to Central America again.

"My brother Kyle—he's a few years older than me— always talked about going to the Far East to teach English and minister there. But my own dreams never quite seemed to jell into anything that resembled a lifetime career of doing the same thing over and over."

"So what'd you do?" Paul asked. He'd settled on the ground, one arm propped on his knee.

Amber smiled, swiftly and then with a touch of lingering sadness. "I did what every American kid daydreams about, but rarely finds—the perfect way to play hooky. I ran away from home."

"You're kidding?"

Shaking her head, she added, "I meant, in a sense. I did everything I was big enough and bad enough to do."

"How old were you then?"

"Two weeks shy of my twentieth birthday. I thought

I knew it all, too. My parents planned for me to go to finish a degree at their Bible-college alma mater. But I backpacked around Mexico for a while, then crossed the border. Hung out in San Diego, then hitchhiked my way to L.A."

"That's very dangerous."

Nodding, she agreed. "And stupid. And childish. So when I met up with a cop who seemed to have it all together—career, faith, finances—I was, like, 'well, see Mom and Pop, I didn't do so bad.'" A shadow crossed her face. "I was twenty-three and everything was right with my world."

When she fell silent, he asked, "Then what happened?"

Amber shrugged. "I found out that looks can be deceiving. I learned that trust isn't something that you can take for granted, that faith without the works to back it up is just a lie. And I found out how many ways you can hurt and not have the pain show."

Loud voices carried from the lodge. They both turned in that direction. Paul was about to ask her what, exactly, she meant, when the sound of a police siren filled the air.

"That's not good. Come on," Paul said, offering a hand to Amber. A moment later, several squad cars filled the compound.

At almost a dead run they sprinted back to the lodge area.

The scene at the teen girls' dorm was a circus. Crying, yelling and name-calling reigned.

An unrepentant-looking Daphne Gregory smirked at the other teens. "Can't you all take a little joke?"

"What you did was dangerous and stupid," somebody yelled, lingering fear making the words sharp. "You could have killed somebody!"

A crowd of campers in various degrees of dress spilled off the porch and into the front yard of the dorm, while others, stragglers who'd heard the sirens and got up to see what the commotion was all about, edged closer.

Inside, the Jackson twins huddled together on a sofa, eyes shooting daggers at Daphne, while the others surrounded them, the young people representing what looked like a united front against Daphne and her cohorts.

"What happened here?" Paul said at the same time as Caleb.

Everyone started talking at once.

"One at a time," Paul said. He didn't know who the dorm parent was, but he saw two people he knew. "Adam? Cindy?"

"Apparently the dispute among these three and the twins wasn't over," the lead counselor explained.

"Daphne and her friends snuck into the room where the twins were and set off firecrackers near their beds," Adam said.

Quick action by Cindy and another counselor had prevented a fire. But they'd called 9-1-1 when Tanita Jackson said she'd been burned and one of the other girls in the room was having trouble breathing.

While the EMTs checked the two girls out, Nancy left to call the parents of the children involved in the fracas. After a nod from Paul, Caleb led Daphne to a squad car.

"Is she going to jail where she belongs?" Tanita demanded hotly.

"We'll let Chief Evans and his officers worry about that," Cliff said.

Nancy returned with a purse and her clipboard. She spoke to Tanita as well as to a girl the EMTs had hooked up to oxygen, just in case. The EMTs cleared them both, declaring fright as the chief problem. Tanita had no visible burns or injuries, but Nancy insisted both girls be looked at further. Their parents would meet them at the hospital.

After a word with Caleb and Paul, Nancy got in the squad car with Daphne. Two parent volunteers rode with the other three girls, the twins clinging to each other.

"It's late," Cliff said, rounding up campers. "I know we all have an early start in the morning, but I'd like to have a word with you."

Suddenly exhausted and still feeling a little raw around the edges, Amber watched Cliff address this latest incident. After a prayer, he dismissed them all.

As the campers headed back to their dorms, Paul turned to Amber. "You're awfully quiet."

"We'd talked earlier," Amber said, her eyes still looking toward the place where the taillights of the emergency vehicles faded away. "I thought things were cool." Sitting in the back of the police car, Daphne didn't look nearly as cocky as she'd been earlier. She'd looked like a scared thirteen-year-old. "What's going to happen to her?"

"Her aunt and uncle—I believe that's who Nancy said were responsible for her—will pick her up at the police station."

"There's always one in the bunch, no matter the place or time. One person who can spoil it for everybody."

Paul heard her, but he wondered if Amber was referring to the incident at the camp, or her own life situation.

As Wayside's police chief, Paul felt duty bound to be at the station to speak with Daphne's guardians and then to check on Tanita and the other girl at the hospital. But first, he'd look in on Jonathan and Sutton. The youngest kids' dorm chaperone stood out front, having kept them all in their bunkhouse.

"Hi there, Chief," Harriet Simmons said. "I should tell you that our little camp is normally very quiet. The biggest thing that's ever happened here was a pack of hot dogs getting burned to a crisp once in a campfire."

"Well, this weekend has certainly been lively."

He climbed the three steps to the porch.

"Did you come to check on the kids? They're sound asleep. Only a couple of them woke up. I remember what it was like to sleep like that."

Paul smiled. "Mind if I peek in on them?"

"Not at all."

A few minutes later, Paul rushed back outside. "They're gone. Jon and Sutton are gone."

"What do you mean *gone?*"

Paul's gaze darted around, looking for likely places where his children might be. "As in, not in their bunks. What happened here, Harriet?"

She clutched her robe tighter. "Nothing. They were... No one left the building. I'd have seen them. Did you check the bathroom? The lounge?"

"They're not in there!"

Harriet stumbled back at the force of his anger and fear.

Paul swiped a hand over his eyes. "I'm sorry. I didn't mean to snap at you."

"What's wrong?" Amber said, pausing in front of the dorm on her way inside.

"Jon and Sutton. They're missing."

"Missing?" Amber grabbed Paul's arm and felt the strength of muscles bunched and tension coiled. "What happened to them?"

"I don't know," Paul said. Running a hand through his hair, he tried to think, tried to figure out what might have spooked them. He slapped his forehead. "Fireworks!"

"What?" Harriet and Amber said at the same time.

"Fireworks going off probably sounded like gunfire to them."

The anguish-filled words, ripped from him, tore at Amber's heart. "We'll find them, Paul. We'll find them. Maybe they just went over to the lodge or to the girls' dorm to see what all the fuss was about."

Harriet dashed inside to look for the siblings herself.

When she returned, she held a walkie-talkie and looked grim. "Their backpacks are gone."

She radioed Cliff and turned to Paul. But he and Amber had already taken off, searching the camp lodge and compound for the two missing children.

"Jon, I'm scared," Sutton said.

"It's safe in here," the boy assured her. "Nobody saw us leave. The bad man won't find us here."

From outside, voices could be heard.

"Shh," Jon said. He held his sister close as the two clutched each other, hiding from the person who'd been shooting up the camp dorm the same way their house in Los Angeles been shot up.

This time it was a real emergency. The police cars they'd heard proved it.

They remained quiet until the voices moved on.

"What if Daddy got shot?"

Jonathan bit his lower lip. He had to be brave. He had to protect his sister. As older brother, that was his job. His mom had told him so.

"He won't," Jon said. But his insides felt trembly and afraid, just like they had *that* night.

"I'm going to search the mess hall," Amber said. "That's where Daphne went to hide."

For the first time since she'd met him, Paul Evans looked truly vulnerable and uncertain. As a man who carried great responsibility not just for himself and his family, but for the entire town, his quick thinking and coolness under fire were attributes that made him a good cop, and an excellent police chief. But the man standing before her now wasn't a cop. He was a father who had just one priority: his children.

"Paul?"

He glanced down as her, his expression grim. "I can't lose them, Amber. Those kids are all I've got left in the world."

Without a word, Amber slipped her hand into his. They stared into each other's eyes for a moment, both realizing the import of what she'd done. Not since Raymond Alvarez had taught her to mistrust all men, particularly men in uniform, had Amber freely given her trust to another human being.

Once he had it, Paul seemed reluctant to let her hand go, as if she, too, might disappear from beneath his nose the way the children had.

"Father God, please keep them safe from hurt, harm and danger."

Paul's prayer, quick and earnest, moved Amber. Her throat constricted.

Cliff and Adam met them in the middle of the compound. Cliff had his walkie-talkie, Adam had a first-aid kit strapped to his waist.

"What's wrong now?" Cliff said. "Harriet said some kids are gone."

"Mine. Sutton and Jonathan. They're not in the dorm."

Adam groaned. "They could be anywhere out here in the dark."

Paul sent a glare in Adam's direction. Amber watched expressions flit across his face before he shut them down, turning into the police chief on an investigation and assignment, rather than a desperate father on a mission.

"They're going to be somewhere where it's safe," he said. "A cave or cubby where they can't be seen."

"That could be a number of places," Adam noted.

"Then, we don't need to waste any more time. Cliff, take the north side. Adam, the south. We'll head in an easterly direction."

"We can cover more ground if I go alone," Amber said. "I'll search that way," she said, indicating the west.

"I don't want to lose you, too." He bent his head, kissed her full and hard on the lips.

Stunned, Amber stood there.

Despite their concern, Cliff and Adam exchanged a smile. "I'll radio for some backup," Cliff said. "Do we need to call your officers again?"

The father in him wanted to yell "yes!" But the police chief knew that a preliminary search needed to be made first. "No," Paul said. "Not yet." He glanced at his watch. "If they're not found in thirty minutes, we'll take the next step."

Watches synchronized, the searchers fanned out.

It took very little in the imagination department for Amber to know just what fear tasted like. Its acrid flavor lingered in her memory. As a child, she'd known fear—of the unknown, of new places, of losing a friend.

As an adult, she'd found new reasons to be afraid. She'd discovered that she gladly would have swapped the fears she'd known as a child for the ones she had been forced to confront as a grown woman.

While the others commenced their segment searches by calling out for Jonathan and Sutton, Amber just stood where she was, revisiting the past.

Once in Guatemala, she'd steered off the trail and found herself lost in lush vegetation so high she couldn't see over it. The night sky, thickly obscured by trees, couldn't help lead her back to camp. She couldn't see the stars. Standing there, she'd felt as if she were quite possibly the only person on Earth. Loneliness almost overwhelmed her eleven-year-old spirit.

She had tried to remember the signs she'd been taught. Moss growing. Brush bent this way or that. But the fear had clawed at her, beating down the survival tactics her parents had insisted she know.

And so she'd sat down, right where she was, in the middle of the jungle. She'd sat down and cried her eyes out.

Now, slowly, Amber opened her eyes and turned around in a slow circle.

Sutton and Jonathan hadn't gone far. She knew it. But just as she'd been well and truly hidden from the search party out looking for her in the jungle, the two children would be hidden in plain view.

She didn't have a watch, but it seemed like maybe five minutes had passed since Paul, Adam and Cliff had started searching. "I know you guys are still here," she said. "Where are you?"

Turning again in a circle in the middle of the compound, she faced two of the camp's outbuildings. Unsure of what was housed in one, Amber headed off in that direction.

Amber's instinct had been right on target. The first building was empty, but in the second one, the boathouse, she'd heard whispering that abruptly stopped.

She passed rows of canoes, stands of oars and footlockers containing life vests. And there, in a corner, sitting between a stack of life preservers, she found two little children.

"May I join you?"

Sutton scrambled up and threw her arms around Amber. "How'd you find us?"

Giving the girl a hug, Amber said, "If I were running away, this would be a pretty good hideout."

Sutton frowned up at Amber, then turned to Jonathan. "We weren't running away. Were we?"

Instead of answering, Jonathan scuffed his tennis shoe on the floor of the boathouse. "You're not my mom."

Taken aback by the comment, Amber shook her head. "No. I'm not. That doesn't mean I don't care about what happens to you."

"Why?" the boy asked.

"Why are you being so mean?" Sutton said, confronting her brother before Amber could answer.

Jonathan got up and stomped away. "All I was trying to do was protect you. Uncle Paul wasn't here. It's my job to protect you."

Amber approached the brave boy who was spoiling for a fight. She placed her hands on his shoulders, felt the tension there, as well as the vulnerability. "You've done a fine job protecting your sister. Tell me, though, Jon, who gets to protect *you?*"

"That's my job," Paul said from the door.

He entered the boathouse, extinguished the flashlight and opened his arms to his children, who propelled themselves straight into his embrace.

"I'm going to need two weeks to recover from this little weekend camping trip," Nancy said later that night.

The Evans children had fallen asleep on the sofa in the common room, their father between them. Amber had excused herself to go bake—what she did best when stressed. So a big batch of honey pecan rolls would probably greet them all in a few hours.

"Maybe I'll treat you to a full day at that spa you love in Portland," said Cliff.

In their room, Nancy smiled at her husband. "That sounds wonderful right about now. This entire weekend has been a disaster from the word go."

"It's not your fault," he said. "You're just focusing on the bad. What about the good?"

In the minister's mind, he counted as good seeing the change in Amber Montgomery. She along with a couple of others remained on his daily prayer list.

"The police have been here—what is it now, three times? Instead of being ambassadors for Christ, we're going to end up with a reputation like the Revelers."

He rubbed her arms, thinking about the switch in perspective. All along, Nancy had been the stalwart, maintaining a cheerful countenance in the midst of all the stress of this year's jamboree. But this latest incident had spooked her well and good.

"I think you're exaggerating just a bit, dear."

Nancy blew out a breath and gave him an exasperated look. "You know what I mean."

He nodded. "Listen, we have just one more day. We'll all eat a hearty breakfast in a few hours. The kids will rehearse their skits. Then we'll have the annual amateur production and go home."

Nancy didn't look as convinced as her husband sounded. "Look at what's gone wrong in just two days. I'm halfway afraid to face tomorrow."

"It's already here," he said. "You have no choice."

"Gee, thanks. Seriously, Cliff. The board needs to discuss this when we get back. Maybe this is a sign that we shouldn't have the jamboree anymore. Maybe we've gotten so focused on doing everything one way that..."

Cliff wrapped his arms around his wife's waist and pulled her close. "Why don't you leave the worrying to the One who has everything under control?"

◈ Chapter Seventeen ◈

Caleb wanted to tell Marnie about the decision that had been placed on his heart. He wanted to hear her ideas about his new venture. He'd yet to figure out how any of this would play in his real life, but for now, at least, after the incident that he liked to refer to as "wrestling with angels until they blessed him," Caleb tried to act nonchalant.

But his heart was beating about seventy miles a minute, just as it had when he was sixteen and asking a girl out for the very first time.

He hadn't known then how to approach Mary Anne Harshont, and now, more than a decade later, he still had no idea how to approach a woman. He loved Marnie with the kind of love that grew deeper by the day—as opposed to the puppy love that he'd felt toward Mary Anne, who grew up to marry a doctor from Bend who knew all the pretty words that seemed to make Caleb tongue-tied. As long as a woman remained his friend, he didn't have any problems talking to her, teasing or even flirting a little. Like he did with Amber.

But when it came to Marnie, Caleb was just a bona fide mess. With Marnie it was all too much, he had too much to say, too much history with Roy, too many things he didn't know...too much that he did know.

And so he suffered in silence.

Maybe Sunday, after church, he figured. He'd go to her house, flowers in hand, and tell her he loved her, tell her how the Lord had laid it on his heart to be a prison chaplain, to minister to incarcerated men and women.

Then, after she kicked him out for reminding her of Roy, he'd go home and lick his wounds and try to mend his broken heart.

The skits went off without a hitch, with only two of the youngest children forgetting their parts. But their teammates helped them out and the Spirit Fire trophy went to the creative effort of a team depicting how faith as small as a mustard seed—portrayed by the silent Sutton Evans holding up a tiny pebble no one could even see—moves mountains.

The one part about the annual jamboree that Nancy Baines didn't like was saying goodbye to everyone. On the one hand, the end of the long weekend meant she could finally breathe and take a well-deserved rest. She planned to hold Cliff to that promise of a day at the spa. Truth be told, though, she anticipated a long soak in a warm tub at home. But before that, she had to bid farewell to all of her charges, the regulars whom they'd expect to see at the same time next year, as well as the scholarship students who'd brought new life, energy, expectations and trouble to the camp.

Now, Nancy watched as the children moved along the closing hug reception line.

"Are you seeing what I'm seeing?" Cliff leaned over and whispered.

All of the camper kids and teens were on one side of the modified receiving line, and all of the parents, volunteers and staff were on the other. From the happy chatter and laughter filling the air as hugs were passed along the line, no one would guess they'd all had a late night. Even the three girls who'd gone to the hospital were among those in the line.

What caught Cliff's attention, and Nancy's, too, was that Chief Evans and Amber had somehow wound up together as they moved through the gauntlet of well-wishers and farewell sayers. Sutton and Jonathan were right in front of them, grinning, jumping to the music that played from a boom box and having a great time.

"I do," Nancy answered her husband. "But I wonder if they see what's so evident to everyone else."

By the time Amber and Paul got to the end of the line where Nancy and Cliff waited to give and receive their own hugs and farewells, Amber's face was flush with laughter.

"Okay, Reverend Baines," she said. "I'll admit this part was fun."

"But not anything else?" Cliff asked, a smile in his voice.

Amber shrugged. "I'll get back to you with that assessment. But for now, just put it this way. The next time Haley and Kara need a backup chef at camp, I'll be busy."

Cliff laughed and gave her a hug anyway.

While Paul shook hands with Cliff, and Sutton and Jonathan got a big hug from Nancy, Amber stepped aside.

She hadn't had fun in the traditional sense this weekend. It seemed she'd been tested the entire time. Physically tested by taking a scary tumble in the water, an incident that now seemed as if it had happened weeks ago instead of in the last forty-eight hours—and tested by faith. She'd taken in a lot this weekend; she'd heard more and considered more than she'd been willing to think about over the past three years.

"You guys ready to load up the truck?"

"And move to Beverly," Amber hummed, finishing the line from one of the television classics she watched on a regular basis.

"I don't wanna leave, Daddy. Can't we stay another day?"

"Yeah, Dad. Let's stay another day," Jonathan concurred. "We can go rock climbing."

Paul crouched down. He smoothed Sutton's hair that had come loose of the band she wore. "The jamboree is over, honey. But, tell you guys what..."

"What?" both kids asked.

"How about on Saturday we go hiking?"

Whoops of joy followed that suggestion. Paul grinned. Yeah, he thought, moving to Oregon was just what they'd all needed.

"Go grab your backpacks and we'll be on our way."

When the kids raced off to claim their gear, Amber was talking to one of the teenagers. Paul watched her and marveled at how much he'd come to enjoy her company.

He wasn't fooled into believing that the intimacy they'd shared in this environment could be replicated once they got home, but he did wonder if Amber would be willing to see him again. He wanted to see her, even as a part of him realized her anger at God and her disdain of the Gospel were obstacles that couldn't be overlooked.

What Paul didn't know was just how much Amber had changed over the weekend. As she hugged Kirsten and then Leanne, promising to keep in touch with the budding chefs, she felt him watching her. His steady gaze, intent and rather disconcerting, seemed focused entirely on her. Amber met his gaze and, for a moment, the air between crackled with an electricity that they neither expected nor knew how to deal with.

"Thanks so much for everything!" Leanne gushed.

Amber blinked, and the moment with Paul was lost.

He cocked his head to the side, looking just as bemused as she felt.

Amber hugged Leanne again.

"I'll see you at church Sunday?" the teenager said.

"Uh…"

Amber saw Paul lean forward, waiting to hear her answer.

"I probably won't make it," Amber said.

She saw Paul's shoulders slump, and felt remorse at something intangible that she seemed to have lost in just that instant.

Two Community Christian Church vans rolled up along with two full-size vans and stopped in front of the lodge. The drivers got out, as did Eunice Gallagher.

"All aboard," she hollered.

As kids started loading into the vans, Eunice walked over and joined Nancy and Cliff.

"Eunice, aren't you a sight for sore eyes," Nancy said.

"I hear it's been lively up there. I missed all the action," the church secretary said.

"How'd the morning services go?" Cliff asked.

"Just fine. That Reverend Henderson kept everybody laughing as he talked about the first time he went fishing. His topic was about being fishers of men."

Cliff nodded. Every fifth Sunday, during the jamboree weekends, and when he and Nancy were on vacation, Community Christian's lead associate minister led the services.

Jonathan and Sutton ran back with their backpacks and duffel bags. "Hi, Mrs. G!" Jonathan called.

"Well, look who's here. Did you two have fun at your first jamboree?"

Both kids nodded.

"Are you going back with me or with your dad?"

Before they could answer, a girl came shrieking out of the woods from one of the trail paths.

All eyes turned in her direction.

"Help me! Help me! I need some help."

On the run, Nancy, Cliff and Paul, along with several of the adults, met her halfway. "Leslie, what's wrong?"

Out of breath, the girl stopped in front of Nancy and Paul, she clutched her side as she bent over. "Daphne. She's gonna jump. You...you gotta h-help her."

A collective gasp filled the air.

Leslie's words and her breathing came out in erratic puffs. "Please. Please. Kevin's trying to make her come down, but...but, sh-she's gonna jump. I just know it."

"Daphne? What is she doing back here?" Nancy said. "I saw her to her house in town. I spoke to her uncle."

"She ran away, caught a ride or something," Leslie said, crying and hiccuping. Tears streamed down the girl's cheeks.

Cliff and Paul stepped into the breach.

"Okay, Leslie," Paul said, bending over the girl. "I want you to catch your breath, okay? You understand?"

The girl nodded.

"We're going to need your help locating Daphne. Do you remember where she is?"

Leslie nodded again.

"All right," Paul said. "That's good. You have to show me just where she is. Do you think you can do that?"

Another nod.

Cliff waved for the van drivers to leave. "Eunice, would you oversee getting all the kids home?"

"Done," the ever-efficient church clerk said.

"D-daddy?" Fear laced Sutton's voice.

Paul paused and turned back to his children. "Dad's going to go to work now, just like I do every day. You guys go home with Mrs. G, and I'll see you soon, okay?"

He looked up at Eunice, who nodded and put her arms around the children's shoulders. "Come along. I'm sure everything here will be just fine. After all, look who's in charge."

She led the children to a van, but they kept turning back to Paul. He was hunched down, listening to Leslie describe where she'd left her friend. Eunice hustled the other children along.

Paul and Cliff quickly determined how they'd handle the situation.

"How did she get back up here?" Nancy asked.

"We can figure that out later," Paul said. "Right now we just need to find her."

"I'll go, too," Amber said.

"Maybe you should…"

"I've talked with Daphne a bit this weekend. Maybe I can talk to her now."

Paul studied her for a quiet moment, then nodded. "Let me grab some stuff from the truck."

He came back from his SUV a moment later with rope, clamps, a first-aid kit and water that he stuffed in a small backpack and shouldered. A braided cord draped across his shoulder and midsection. He handed Nancy a walkie-talkie and jammed a portable police radio in a pocket, then tugged on a pair of scuffed but sturdy gloves.

"We'll call as soon as we can. If it looks like we need more help, I'll tell you what to do."

Nancy nodded. "Be careful."

They huddled for a quick but earnest prayer, and then Paul, Cliff and Amber took off, following Leslie.

↦ Chapter Eighteen ↤

It took almost twenty minutes of hiking to get to the site. Amber recognized the lookout bluff where she and Marnie had talked the other day. Marnie had been concerned about her safety, and Amber was a grown woman who regularly worked out. About fifty yards beyond that point, through a break in the trees, they spied a flash of color.

"There they are," Leslie said. She ran ahead, calling for Kevin.

"I came up here the other day," Amber said. "There's a ledge right off the side of the cliff. You can easily get to it, but coming back up might be tricky."

"How wide?" Paul asked.

"About four feet."

He said something under his breath that she couldn't make out.

A few moments later, they reached the spot. Kevin,

lying on the ground, dangled his hand over the edge of a precipice.

"Oh, boy," Cliff said.

Surveying the area, Paul had to agree with the bleak assessment. If a path existed, he couldn't see it. The area, narrow and scrabbly, didn't offer much room to maneuver. He shrugged off the backpack.

Kevin glanced back at them. Concern etched the boy's face. None of the earlier cockiness the three children had displayed while scuffling with the other campers showed. The boy was scared.

"She's down there," he said.

"Who are you talking to?" Daphne demanded, her voice small but still laced with vehement disdain.

"Uh, it's that preacher. And the cop."

"Cop!" The girl swore. "Go away. I don't want you here. I got nothing to say to you."

"All right, Daphne," Paul said.

He unzipped the pack and pulled out the rope, testing its tensile strength and length. He looked around, but none of the trees in this area looked sturdy enough to serve as an anchor.

"Daphne, we came up to see about you," Cliff said.

"There ain't nothing to see," the girl said. "You kicked me out."

Amber, Paul and Cliff shared a look.

"Daph, you're scaring me," Leslie said. She'd sat cross-legged on the ground near Kevin, who continued at his prone post at the edge. "Why are you doing this?"

"Shut up, Leslie," Daphne said.

Leslie jumped up. "Fine. I don't care what you do. Jump. Go ahead and jump. Nobody cares."

"That's not true," Amber said, her voice quiet but filled with conviction. "Leslie, leave us alone for a minute."

Leslie stormed off down the mountainside, kicking up stones and brush in her wake.

"Who's that?" Daphne demanded.

Paul motioned for Amber to get closer, to talk to the girl.

"It's me," Amber said. "Amber Montgomery, the cook."

"Jesus, what'd Leslie do? Bring the whole camp up here?"

Kevin rolled over to give Amber some room, then scrambled up. He went straight to Cliff, who had his arms open wide to accept the boy whose face was streaked with dirt and tears.

Paul wrapped the rope around his waist and tied a knot. Then he used one of the clamps to secure it to the end of the cording he'd draped over his neck and shoulder.

"Leslie's gone," Amber said. "It's just me and some people who want to help you."

"I don't need any help," the girl said.

But a trickle of pebbles tumbled down and what sounded like a whimper floated up toward Amber.

"I used to think that, too," Amber said.

She looked over her shoulder at Cliff and Paul. Cliff was tending to scratches and scrapes on the boy's hands and knees, while Paul had edged into the thicket, the radio at his mouth as he tried to get a message through to the camp without alerting Daphne.

Amber faced the edge again, then got down on the ground, prone the way Kevin had been. "I used to think nobody cared about me."

"I don't think it, I know it," Daphne said. "Nobody wants me."

"I bet that's not true," Amber said, even as she prayed it wasn't. With a start she realized she'd been praying from the moment Leslie burst into the compound saying Daphne was in trouble. As a matter of fact, she'd been praying all weekend.

Lord, give me the words to help her. Keep her safe, please.

"Nobody likes me at school. And nobody likes me at this stupid camp."

"Did I tell on you when you were in the kitchen?" Amber asked. "Did I turn you in?"

Silence greeted those questions.

"Friends look out for each other," Amber said. "Kevin and Leslie were concerned enough about you to call for some help. We don't want to see anything happen to you, Daphne. Especially me."

"Why?" The question was small and wary.

Amber had been through the same things as this young girl. She'd found herself in an unbearable situation with Raymond, and the only way out had been to take herself out of the game, to declare defeat and just end it all.

Then, like now, Amber wasn't quite sure where her strength came from, but she knew this troubled young teenager needed to hear that others carried burdens, if not identical to her own, just as heavy.

"Because I was once just like you," Amber said. "I was a little older, but I was considering doing the same thing you're considering."

"You were gonna jump off a mountain?"

"No," Amber said. "I was going to shoot myself in the head with my boyfriend's gun."

Paul's head whipped up. Cliff dropped the antiseptic spray he was holding.

But all of Amber's concentration was on the thirteen-year-old with the grown-up problems.

"How come you were gonna do that?"

"The guy I was seeing then, my boyfriend, he beat me up all the time," Amber said.

Daphne sniffled. "My uncle hits me, too."

"It hurts, doesn't it," Amber said.

"Yeah." But the word was clouded by snuffles indicating Daphne was crying. "I hate living there. He makes me do things. In the dark. He tried last night and I ran away."

Amber's heart went out to the girl. Instinctively, though, she knew not to say any of the platitudes that people usually offered up. "It's not your fault, Daphne," she said simply. "And you don't have to take it anymore."

Amber realized that what she said was true, not just for Daphne, but for herself as well.

"He curses at me and hits me, then he..." Daphne started crying in earnest then, the sound pitiful.

Amber's own tears fell. *Lord, tell me what to do.*

"It's going to be all right, Daphne. The Lord loves you, and so do I. You're gonna get through today, and then tomorrow and the next day and the next. And every day is going to be better than the one before. I promise."

The words came from a place Amber didn't even know existed. She didn't know how or why she said what she did, but in her heart of hearts, she knew that it would work out for Daphne.

And if she did nothing else, she'd make sure that that man paid for what he'd done to the girl, just like Raymond Alvarez was paying for what he'd done to Amber.

Amber started when Paul tapped her on the shoulder. She looked back and up. He stood with the ropes, a lasso made to haul Daphne up.

"Daphne?"

No answer.

Amber peered over the edge. Loose stones fell.

A whimper sounded from below.

"Daphne?"

"Uh-huh?"

"I'm going to send down a rope for you. Will you take it so I can get you up?"

"No."

Amber cast stricken eyes up at Paul. He moved his hands in a rolling motion for Amber to keep talking.

"We can talk better up here."

"I'm not going back there."

"And nobody's going to make you," Amber said.

"They did before."

"It won't happen again," Amber insisted. "I'm going to see to it myself."

"Leslie said that big cop was up there. He wants to take me to jail."

"You're not going to jail," Paul said, his voice as level and soothing as if he were tucking a sleepy Sutton into bed. "Why would we take you to jail? We're going to get you some help."

"I don't believe you. Cops lie."

"Yeah," Amber said, her attention back on the girl. "Some of them do. The boyfriend who used to beat me up all the time was a cop. He thought he could get away with it because of his position. But what he did to me was wrong, just like what your uncle is doing to you is wrong. We can put a stop to it, Daphne. But you've got to help."

"How?"

"Well, first we've got to get you up from there."

A piece of the ledge gave way, and Daphne screamed.

Paul tossed the rope to Cliff. "We've got to hurry. I radioed for a helicopter, but it'll take at least another forty minutes to get here from Portland. We don't have that much time."

"Show me what to do," Cliff said.

"Hold on, Daph. I'm coming for you," Amber said.

"Argh!" came up from where Daphne was trapped.

Amber leaned over, and more rocks tumbled. Paul pulled her back.

"I can't have you falling, too." He tugged on the rope, then made a lasso. "Daphne, I'm going to send a rope to you. I want you to put it over your head, settle it under your arms and tug it."

"I can't."

"What do you mean, you can't."

Amber pushed at him. "She's already scared enough. You're gonna freak her out." To Daphne she said, "It's okay. I know you can do it."

She turned to Paul. "Let me. I'll go down there, get her secured, and you and Cliff can pull us both up."

Paul mentally weighed the risks. It was too dangerous to lower Amber to the ledge that was already showing signs of strain.

"It's not safe," he said.

"What can I do?" Kevin said.

Paul had forgotten about the boy. "Mrs. Baines is directing the rescue workers up here. Can you go meet them? Show them where we are?"

Kevin nodded, earnest in his mission. "Daphne, it's gonna be okay," he called out. "We're all gonna get you."

"Okay" came a small, scared voice. "I think you better hurry."

Kevin tore off through the brush down the mountain.

Amber figured she knew just as much if not more than

Paul about wilderness survival. And this sure looked like a survival mission.

"Lower me down and I'll pull her back up."

Paul shook his head. "It's too dangerous."

"I weigh a lot less than you do," she pointed out. "It'll work."

Paul knew she was right, but he didn't like it. Not one bit.

He took the rope from around his waist and put it over Amber's head and shoulders. After securing it, he kissed her hard and fast. "Be careful."

"I will."

With Paul and Cliff acting as anchors, she got on the ground and edged over the side of the cliff.

With Amber dangling over the side of the mountain, rocks and grasses broke away.

Daphne shrieked in terror.

Amber tossed the lasso she carried with her over the girl's head. She could see the crack in the ledge as the ground began to break away. "Pull it down, Daphne, pull it down around you."

Daphne reached for the rope.

The ledge gave way.

ᴓ Chapter Nineteen ᴓ

Amber didn't know who yelled louder in that instant—she, Daphne, Cliff or Paul. She'd been scared before, but never, ever, like that. In one agonizingly long moment, she thought she'd lost Daphne, that she herself was also tumbling head over heels down the jagged cliff side and into the raging waters below.

But Cliff and Paul dug in, holding fast.

After the rescue, no one talked during the trip down the mountain, with Daphne on a stretcher that had been hauled up by the EMTs. When they emerged through the trees, a crowd waited at the camp. Word had gotten out in town, and Community Christian Church members, teenagers and worried parents flocked to the camp. A hospital helicopter whirred in a clearing.

A cheer went up when Paul said no one had life-threatening injuries. Daphne had suffered a gash on her leg from a root that scraped her as they'd hauled her up. Cliff had rope burns on his hands. And all four of them bore myriad scrapes and scratches. But they were all safe.

Amber and Paul, both obstinate, insisted they were fine and didn't need to go to the hospital. But despite Cliff's objections, an anxious Nancy insisted he get his hands checked.

While a reporter and photographer from the *Wayside Gazette* snapped pictures and asked questions of some of the teens, Amber slipped away. Spying her, Paul followed.

Even now, safe and secure at the compound, Amber felt adrenaline racing through her veins. She walked in circles, flexing her hands. She wanted to run, to scream, to hit something.

"Walk it off," Paul said.

She whirled around. "Huh?"

"Come on," he said, grabbing her hand. "Walk it off. I can see the pent-up energy pulsing in you. It's like that with near-death experiences."

"I need to run."

"Let's go, then." And so they took off, silent but together. By mutual but unspoken agreement, they headed toward the entrance of the camp rather than the acreage so thoroughly explored over the long weekend. After the third mile, Amber was starting to feel better—and a little silly.

"Thank you," she said, as they jogged along the roadside.

Sparse traffic traveled along the road leading to the camp on this mid-afternoon in early fall. The rest of the day promised to be cool but comfortable.

They eventually slowed to a walk as they again approached the camp entrance. "This has been one long three-and-a-half-day weekend. It seems like we've been up here at least a month."

Paul chuckled. "Time is like that, especially when a lot is going on." They were quiet for a moment. Then, he said, "Amber, I realize now that what happened in the water and the other day while we were hiking together... Well, I want to apologize for my behavior."

"You have nothing to apologize for," she said.

"From the moment we met, all I've done is manhandle you in some way, shape or form," he said. "I see now that I could have managed every one of those situations in a better way."

"I don't usually talk about what happened to me in L.A.," Amber told him. "The life I had there is stuff I want to banish from my memory banks. It's just taken me a little longer than I would have expected or liked."

"What you told Daphne on that mountain saved her life."

"You and Cliff Baines saved her life," Amber said. "You two were the ones pulling. If you hadn't been pulling like crazy, we'd all be dead or seriously injured right now."

Paul shook his head, disagreeing with her as she discounted her own efforts to save Daphne. "I don't think there are any coincidences in this life, Amber. Everything on this earth happens for a reason. Even if we can't see or touch or even know the reason or discover the impact, there's still a reason."

"Like me meeting Jon and Sutton at Sunshine and Rainbows?"

He nodded. "You were meant to be here today, to help that girl. I couldn't have talked her down. Neither could Cliff. We had nothing to offer her." He ran a hand through his hair. "Shoot, if it had just been us up there, she probably would have jumped. Your experience is what she could relate to. You gave her hope."

Not comfortable with the praise, Amber didn't say anything.

"I wish I could get my hands on that cop who hurt you," he said.

"He's probably out of prison and beating up somebody else now."

"But you're here," Paul said. "Don't you think God had a hand in that?"

Amber shrugged, not willing to confess to him that she'd been having the same thoughts.

The God she'd believed abandoned her in Los Angeles had always been there, sheltering her, preparing her. If not for this day and that young girl, for a greater purpose that he had yet to reveal for her life.

She glanced at the man next to her. Over the past few days, she'd come to think of him as more than a lug-head cop. As more than just another man who had the potential to hurt her. Not every police officer was like Raymond Alvarez.

She'd borne witness to the fact that there were, indeed, Christian men who were strong believers, who lived their faith, walked it and talked it even while going about their normal lives.

Growing up, she'd thought of her parents, particularly her father, as a Bible thumper, but she now realized that the particular calling on her parents' lives meant they had to be bold in their faith.

Amber didn't know if she was ready to be bold, but she was ready to make a new commitment to walk in the light. To trust God the way she used to. She looked at her feet, the hiking boots. "Trust in the Lord with all your heart, And lean not on your own understanding; In all your ways acknowledge Him, And He shall direct your paths." He'd surely directed their paths today.

Considering Paul's words, Amber realized that everything so far in her life *had* been leading to this moment, this day. What part did the man next to her have in it all?

"You kissed me back there."

He nodded. "I did."

"Actually, that was the second time this weekend."

The first time, when they'd gone in search of the missing Jonathan and Sutton, she'd been too stunned to think about what that might mean. And up on that mountain, she hadn't had time to process anything except the crisis at hand.

"Why?"

It was Paul's turn to contemplate his feet. "Why did I kiss you?"

He was stalling for time because, in all honesty, he didn't know. "I... Amber, to level with you, I don't know. I didn't plan to either time." He shrugged. "What made me do it? Maybe it had something to do with the adrenaline factor of both situations."

She studied his face. Those Mediterranean-blue eyes were filled with questions, many of the same ones that she herself had. She checked her pulse, then reached for his arm and checked his.

Paul smiled. "What are you doing?"

"The adrenaline factor isn't an issue right now. My heartbeat is back to normal. Yours, too."

He nodded. "And?"

"And I just wanted to make sure that there was nothing going on that this could be blamed on."

He opened his mouth to ask what she was talking about, but Amber placed an open palm on his chest and leaned forward. She didn't let herself think beyond this moment, this single irrational act. All Amber knew was that she wanted to kiss Paul, to have him hold her for just a moment, to be able to believe, if only for this snapshot in time, that she had worth and value and beauty to share.

She pressed her lips to his and felt his arm encircle her waist.

She quivered at the sweet tenderness of his touch.

Marveled at how she felt like a flower blossoming after days without the sun or rain.

And then, she stepped away.

"I need to go."

"But..."

Amber didn't give him a chance to say anything else. She dashed up the drive, leaving Paul standing at the entrance to Camp Spirit Fire, cherishing the precious, precious gift he'd just been given.

For the last time, Amber glanced back at the Community Christian Church camp. She'd taken the job to help Haley and Kara out, as well as to boost her business's bottom line. But over the course of the long weekend, she'd found something far more valuable than an hourly wage payable at triple rate.

She'd found the way home.

Wise words from the Old Testament came to mind: "Train up a child in the way he should go and when he is old, he won't depart from them." After years of running, years of believing that God didn't care a whit about her, Amber realized that He'd never stopped caring, never stopped loving her, even though she'd turned her back on Him.

"Forgive me, Lord," she said out loud.

And instantly, she was delivered, set free and made whole.

Her voice seemed to echo in the van, but Amber sat focused on the joy bubbling up through her spirit and soul. Tears streamed down her face. "Thank you, Lord. Thank you."

She wasn't sure just how long she sat there. Maybe until her tears dried. Maybe until her spirit was completely renewed.

As she reached for the keys to start the ignition, a knock sounded at the window.

Paul stood there, concern on his face. "Are you okay? Do you need a jump?"

Amber looked at him, a grin slowly spreading on her face. Then she opened her door and jumped out. "I'm better than okay," she said. "I'm fabulous!" She threw her arms around his neck.

Laughing, caught up in her enthusiasm, Paul smiled as he clasped her about the waist to avoid them both taking a tumble to the ground.

Amber, laughing and crying at the same time, tried to tell him. Tried to get all the words out. But there was too much. Too much joy. Too much relief that she was once again in the safe arms of the Lord.

She pressed a kiss to his cheek and hugged him close. "Thank you!"

Paul hugged her back. "For what?"

She spread her arms wide. "For this."

Paul's brows creased. "I know it's been a pretty traumatic day. Is this your celebration that it's all over?"

She cupped his cheek with the palm of her hand and gazed into his kind blue eyes. "Yes. And no."

She grabbed his hand, shook it as if he were a stranger

she'd just met, then turned to her van. "There's something I have to do."

A bemused Paul just stared at her.

A moment later, she gunned the engine and sped down the drive. About fifteen minutes after that, the enormity of what she was about to do hit her. She eased up on the gas as she turned onto the familiar street—one she'd studiously avoided for three years.

Everything looked the same, and it all looked different. The grass somehow seemed greener, but the houses smaller. With a start, Amber realized that she'd never really viewed this street—one house in particular— through adult eyes. She wondered if everything about the house and the yard would also be just as it was in her memory.

Her bedroom in the house featured wallpaper with little pink and green flowers, a desk under the window. A straw doll, given by Angeline as a farewell gift, would be on her pillow. That doll was the one thing she'd missed having with her all these years.

In the time since she'd returned to Wayside, Amber had actively avoided her parents. Helen Montgomery had made overtures, had attempted to bridge the divide that separated them, but Amber had rebuffed every attempt at reconciliation. Even so, every year on her birthday and at Christmas, a card arrived, signed by both her parents. Each one carried two things: a familiar Bible verse, and a message from them—*We love you, Amber.*

If she hadn't known better, she'd have been willing to

bet real money that Helen and Richard Montgomery arranged with Pastor Cliff to use Proverbs 3:5-6 as a Scripture text at the camp.

"In all your ways acknowledge Him, And He shall direct your paths."

He shall direct your path. Amber laughed nervously at that. When she'd awakened this morning, it hadn't been with the intention that she'd stop a girl from jumping off a cliff, or reunite with her parents.

Rededicating her life to the Lord was one thing. Showing up on Helen and Richard Montgomery's front doorstep was another altogether.

She hesitated. Then, climbing out of the van and heading up the walk before she completely lost her nerve, she muttered, "What do you have to lose?"

Reaching out a tentative hand, Amber glanced back at her van. She could be out of here and they'd never even know she'd stopped by.

Her heart was racing as if she'd been running.

She was struck by the realization that she had, indeed, been running. All of her life. Running away from unpleasant truths, running away from Raymond Alvarez, running away from her own fears.

It was time to face all of those fears head-on. As long as she kept them bottled inside, instead of dissipating, they grew into out-of-control monsters that threatened to consume her.

Taking a deep, cleansing breath, Amber pressed the doorbell.

* * *

Caleb figured it was now or never.

At some point a man had to face the unpleasant truth. He had to tell Marnie how he felt. Even if she spurned him, even if she said he was despicable for loving his brother's wife and told him she never wanted to see him again, he had to take this next step. If he didn't, he thought he just might explode.

He'd been too embarrassed to talk to his pastor or any of his friends about Marnie. And he sure wasn't about to bring it up with Roy.

Caleb pulled his pickup truck into the drive, skirting the tree trunk. Marnie's grass was a little higher than normal. He made a mental note to swing by later and mow the lawn for her.

Clearing his throat and ignoring the knot in his gut, he knocked at the front door.

A moment later, she opened it, her smile growing wide when she saw him.

"Hi, Caleb. Come on in. I was just thinking about you."

His hopes soared. "You were?"

He followed her into the house.

And stopped cold when he saw the boxes in the living room. Plastic bubble wrap and newspapers were stacked at the ready in the easy chair.

"What's going on?"

"I'm leaving."

His heart slammed into his chest. "What do you mean leaving?"

She went to the sofa and sat down, patting the cushion beside her. Photo albums lay open on the coffee table in front of the couch. Caleb glanced at a picture of the three of them—himself, Marnie and Roy—at a basketball game in Portland. He remembered the night well: the Trailblazers won the game and he'd acknowledged that his feelings for Marnie went much deeper than appropriate given the fact that she and Roy were married.

Marnie tucked a leg under her on the cushion and faced him, excitement racing over her features. "I'm going to Coos Bay," she told him. "I've been offered a job and I've given it a lot of thought. I'm going to take it."

"Coos Bay? That's three or four hours from here."

She nodded, reached for his hands. "Caleb, I'm so excited. I realized this weekend that there's nothing holding me here. Nothing except bad memories. I'm going to go down there and start over."

But I'm here, he wanted to say. *We can start good memories together. Just the two of us.*

But he didn't say the words. Instead, he bit back bitter disappointment. Maybe they just weren't meant to be.

"You deserve that," he told her. "You deserve every happiness."

Marnie leaned back in the sofa cushions and closed her eyes. "I can't believe I'm doing this," she said. She sat up again and grinned. "But it feels so good. Of course, I have to give notice at Sunshine and Rainbows. And find a place to live down there, and get my stuff shipped. But, oh, Caleb, I'm so happy."

She threw her arms around him, and Caleb closed his eyes, savoring the closeness, the light citrus scent of her perfume, her soft curves, the texture of her hair. He inhaled it all, delighting in the moment, storing up the memories that he'd need to get him through the days, weeks and months without her near.

"I'm happy for you, too, Marnie."

But Caleb closed his eyes and prayed he wouldn't start crying.

❦ Chapter Twenty ❦

"Is Amber going to be our mommy?"

Sutton and Jonathan were in Sutton's room, sitting on her bed. It had been a week since they'd returned from jamboree, and the day after a cool hiking trip, but they were still talking about the church camp weekend, Amber in particular.

"She can't be," Jonathan told his sister. "We already have a mommy."

"But I don't remember her," Sutton said. "I want a mom like everybody else. Susie's mom bakes her cookies that look like her doll. And Kenyatta's mom braids her hair." Sutton fingered her ponytail—all Paul could manage by way of styling a five-year-old's hair. "If I had a mommy, she'd braid my hair."

Jonathan pouted. "What do you need a mom for?"

Sutton looked at her brother as if he'd just sprouted two heads. "For just about everything," she said.

Paul stood at the door of Sutton's bedroom. He'd been about to roust them out and downstairs for breakfast, but their conversation stopped him cold. He paused, not quite sure how to approach the children.

He liked Amber—a lot. In the week since they'd been home, he'd thought of little else but the woman who'd placed a hand over his heart and pressed her lips to his.

He'd seen Amber in that week. She'd followed through on her promise to Daphne. The girl and her younger brother were both in the care of a loving foster family, one that Cliff Baines recommended and knew. The circumstances of the children's home life with their aunt and uncle was the stuff of case studies. But with an outraged Amber as an advocate, and both Paul and Reverend Baines as witnesses to what a frightened Daphne said on that mountain, justice would be served on behalf of the girl and her brother.

But each time he'd seen Amber in public, she had acted as if he were nothing but the town's police chief. He'd tried to see her, had even stopped by her place a couple of times, but Amber was either busy with catering orders or on the way to her parents' house.

He knew that what had happened at Camp Spirit Fire had been an aberration, a moment out of time that had no bearing on the reality they all lived. Still, all week, Paul's thoughts had been on Amber.

His prayers for guidance seemed to go unheeded, and now, here sat Jonathan and Sutton dissecting his life—their lives.

Any woman who became a part of his life would also become part of his children's lives. That's why he'd all but stopped dating after Mikey and Sarah died—that and the grief...compounded with the guilt.

Through the group counseling sponsored by the police department, he'd finally been able to accept that he wasn't to blame for their deaths. If it hadn't been Mikey and Sarah, it would have been someone else. But a part of him never let go of the fact that it *was* his fault.

He loved these two children more than anything in the world and he wouldn't risk their already fragile emotional well-being just because he wanted some companionship. The women he had met and dated before the shooting weren't the type interested in a ready-made family. And the ones he'd met afterward—mostly in grief counseling—had had just as much mental baggage as he did. The last thing he needed was somebody else's drama and crisis points while he still worked through his own.

So he'd just skipped the whole dating thing and any thought of it. Until now. He'd moved to Wayside in part to find a woman with godly values who could accept him and the children with love. Instead of finding a morph of housewife stereotypes, though, he'd fallen for a skittish caterer who had just as many issues as he did—maybe more. Despite what he'd thought he wanted, the Lord had had another vision.

Except that now it looked like maybe Amber *wasn't* the one.

Granted, he knew very little about Amber Montgomery, and the part he did know was enough to send a sane man running in the opposite direction. He'd checked up on Raymond Alvarez, and what he'd found still made his blood boil. But Paul wanted to get to know Amber, to go out on a normal date—one that didn't involve half drowning in a raging river or clinging to the side of a collapsing cliff.

It had just been a week, and a busy one at that, but he could take a hint. She'd kissed him with sweet tenderness up at Camp Spirit Fire, but that kiss, he now realized, had been a rite of passage for her, not a declaration of intent or desire for more.

"Hey, guys," he said in greeting.

The children looked up, guilty expressions on their faces as if they'd been caught doing something wrong.

"Hi, Daddy."

"What are you guys talking about? You're looking awfully serious and glum for a cheery Sunday morning."

"Nothing, Daddy," Sutton said, but she cast a quick glance at Jonathan.

"Nothing, Uncle Paul."

Paul raised a brow at that. He doubted that Jonathan even realized that the only time he referred to Paul as "uncle" was when he was sleepy or angry. Since the children were both fully dressed and wide awake, Paul knew he had an issue to deal with. One that couldn't wait.

"Nothing, huh?" he said, entering the room and settling on the edge of Sutton's bed. The girl climbed into his lap. "I heard you guys talking about Amber."

Sutton looked at Jonathan, and then at Paul. "I want Amber to be my mommy, but Jon says she can't 'cause we already have a mom."

"Yes," Paul said. "You do have a mom. But she's in heaven with Jesus, looking out for you."

Sutton gave Jon a "so-there" tongue poke.

Paul tapped her leg. "None of that."

"Are you gonna marry Amber?" Jon asked the question with a belligerent tone, his chin poked out.

Paul realized he needed to be totally honest with them on this. Any decision he made would also have an impact on their lives.

"It's crossed my mind," he told them. "But when and if—and that's a big if—I ever get married, whomever marries me, marries you, too. We're a team. A package deal, and nobody's ever going to change that."

Sutton raised a hand and brushed at the corner of his eyes. "Daddy, you look sad."

Was the girl clairvoyant as well? "We had a long weekend and it's been a busy week. Plus, you wore me out yesterday on that trail."

She stared at him for a bit, as if willing the truth from him. Then, like the five-year-old she was, her attention wandered. "Jon says he didn't like the camp."

"I didn't say that."

"Yes, you did."

"I didn't," the boy said in his own defense. "What I said was, I didn't like the way we had to hurry up and eat. Nobody got to savor their meals."

Paul's brow wrinkled. "Savor their meals? Where'd you hear that?"

"Amber says that's what people should do when they eat," Sutton reported.

Paul grinned. "Well, she's right. How would you guys like to savor some spaghetti after church?"

Their cheers told him he'd picked a winner for dinner. But Paul felt a lingering need to explain about Amber.

"If I ever decide to get serious about someone, she'll have to meet with your approval. You're more important to me than anyone else."

Sutton frowned. "But we don't want someone else. We want Amber!"

Paul looked at Jonathan, who nodded his agreement.

Paul wanted Amber, too. But he was afraid that Amber didn't want him.

The eleven o'clock service at Community Christian Church was jammed. Extra chairs were brought out and placed along the back row. The Sunday after the jamboree was always packed. Kids went home, told their parents and friends about the camping weekend, and both services had an overflowing congregation. But the end of this year's jamboree had been anything but normal.

The *Wayside Gazette* had done three articles about the

mountain rescue of Daphne Gregory and the heroic effort to save her by the pastor, the police chief and the Cookie Lady. Young Kevin even had his picture in the paper showing how he'd led the EMTs to the spot.

During the weekend, several young people had come forward during the campfire invitations, and this was their first exposure to the formal church. So they and all their families were also in attendance.

Matt Brandon-Dumaine led the inspirational choir through two hand-clapping selections. Then Cliff got up. Today he wore a robe, instead of the jeans and light sweaters he'd donned in the woods.

"Welcome to Family and Friends Day at Community Christian," he said. "We're delighted to have all of you with us this morning. And let me just tell you this, we are *truly glad* to be here!"

A cheer went up among the congregation.

He asked all of the people who had spent the weekend at jamboree and those who had helped prepare for the camp to stand. Applause, loud and long, sounded out in the sanctuary.

Near the back, in the only place they'd been able to find seats, Paul and the children clapped with the others and then settled again in their pew.

Sutton motioned for Paul. As he leaned down so she could whisper in his ear, someone slipped into the seat next to him.

"We have many things to thank God for this day," Cliff said. "At this time I'd like everyone to take a few moments to reflect on the goodness of the Lord. As you take the hand of your neighbor, bow your heads and close your eyes for a moment of individual thanks."

Jonathan took Sutton's hand. On Paul's left, Sutton put her small hand in her dad's. And Paul extended his right to the person next to him. He glanced over and his eyes widened.

Amber.

Their gazes held, and then she smiled.

"Hey," she said.

"Hey."

This day had been a long time coming, but Amber had no doubt she'd made the right decision. In private she'd rededicated her life to the Lord. Now, by coming to church again, she'd make the public profession of faith. And maybe, just maybe, she'd step into the light of a new relationship with a man who loved the Lord as much as she did.

As Cliff began a congregational prayer of thanks, Amber put her hand in Paul's. Then, her gaze holding his eyes, she laced her fingers with his.

When he gently squeezed and lifted their joined hands to press a kiss to the back of her hand, Amber knew she had yet another thing to be thankful for.

What would happen next between them would be revealed as time passed and they got to know each other. For now, though, Amber's spirit overflowed with joy.

Sweet peace filled her. The Lord had brought her

through the trials in L.A., and the danger of this weekend, all the while keeping her safe.

He'd seen her reunited with her parents, and now with Paul, He'd provided the potential of something more, something she welcomed because she'd never thought she'd have it in her life: the sweet devotion of a God-fearing man and the love of two beautiful children.

Thanking God for all His many blessings, Amber smiled and bowed her head in prayer.

∝ *Author Note* ∝

In the time since my first Love Inspired novel was published, I've received many, many letters asking about Amber, who was introduced in *Sweet Accord*. What happened to her? Did she ever find hope and healing? Will she have her own story? Amber did find her way home, literally and spiritually. I hope you enjoyed reading about her journey.

In addition to spiritual guidance, Amber needed a physical guide, someone she could trust who would understand her fears without judging her. In *Sweet Devotion*, Marnie Shepherd served in that role for Amber. But real-life women who are in crisis need a friend as well.

If you or someone who know or love is in need of a friend, a listening ear, there is help available. Domestic violence takes many forms. It can be physical, emotional, verbal or sexual. If you're not sure whether what you're seeing or experiencing is domestic violence, there are organizations across the country that can answer your questions. They cater especially to women who have been abused.

If you'd like more information for yourself or someone you know, call the National Domestic Violence Hotline at 1-800-799-SAFE (1-800-799-7233). It's a toll-free call, and someone is available twenty-four hours a day to offer crisis intervention, referrals to local agencies and help in finding resources. You can also log on to www.ndvh.org for more information.

Thank you for reading *Sweet Devotion*. I enjoy hearing from readers, so if you'd like to write, I can be reached at P.O. Box 1438, Dept. LI, Yorktown, VA 23692. If you are able, please enclose a self-addressed stamped envelope for a prompt reply.

May God's blessings and peace shine on you.

Still Waters

**A stunning debut novel of love,
intrigue and newfound faith.**

Gang terror shatters the sleepy town of Lakeview, Virginia,
and Tiffany Anderson suddenly becomes the target of
a violent crime.

Can Sheriff Jake Reed move beyond the hurts of his past to
solve the crime and save the woman God has meant for him?

SHIRLEE McCOY

Available in January 2004, wherever books are sold!

Steeple
Hill ®

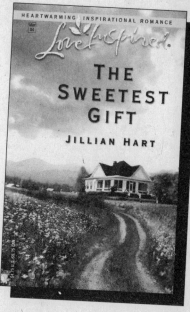

Love Inspired

THE SWEETEST GIFT

BY

JILLIAN HART

Pilot Sam Gardner was next-door neighbor and a friend to Kirby McKaslin when she needed one…and the man she fell in love with. But Sam was the one who needed Kirby to convince him that, despite his painful past, he could have a wonderful future—with her as his wife!

Don't miss

THE SWEETEST GIFT

On sale March 2004

Available at your favorite retail outlet.

Love Inspired ™ ®

SECOND CHANCE AT LOVE

BY

IRENE BRAND

Years ago, their young marriage was torn apart by tragedy and infidelity. Yet former college sweethearts—and now Christians—Amelia Stone and Chase Ramsey were reunited while helping out victims of a severe flood. Was God giving this special couple a second chance at love?

Don't miss

SECOND CHANCE AT LOVE
On sale March 2004

Available at your favorite retail outlet.